I0541199

JONATHAN STURAK

GLOBAL

BURNING

A POST-APOCALYPTIC NOVEL

PENDAN PUBLISHING

Published in the United States of America by Pendan Publishing

The Library of Congress has catalogued the paperback edition as follows:

Sturak, Jonathan

Global Burning : A Novel / by Jonathan Sturak

p. cm.

ISBN: 978-0-9825-8949-6

www.sturak.com

For Jack

About the author:

Jonathan Sturak grew up in the Pocono Mountains of Pennsylvania. He is a Penn State University graduate and holds degrees in Computer Science and Film. He currently lives in Las Vegas where he uses the energy of the city to craft stories about life and the human condition. *The Place Called Home*, Sturak's essay about Eastern European heritage in Northeast Pennsylvania, was featured on *Glass Cases*, literary agent Sarah LaPolla's pop culture blog. Sturak is also a contributing editor at NoirNation.com, the premier location for international crime fiction. His debut thriller novel *Clouded Rainbow* was published in December 2009 and has over 200,000 downloads on the Amazon Kindle. Sturak keeps updated information on his website at sturak.com

Also by the Author

NOVELS
Geek vs Vegas
His First, Her Last
Vegas Was Her Name
A Smudge of Gray
Clouded Rainbow

COLLECTIONS
From Vegas With Blood

STORIES
Don't Kill the Camel
Feed Me!

GLOBAL

BURNING

Nature does nothing in vain.

—Aristotle

Prologue

Steam swirls above a coffee cup. The skinny cameraman takes a sip, but the heat scalds his lips.

"No drinks allowed," the curvaceous camerawoman next to him says.

He sets the coffee down and tightens the locks on his tripod.

A hundred cameras fill the room. Men and women in suits sit in chairs. Some have notepads, while others have tablet computers or digital voice recorders. At the corners of the room, men in black suits sweep the floor with their eyes.

"Are you freelance?" the skinny cameraman asks the woman.

"Do I look like I'm freelance?"

He notices her black polo shirt, crisped, with the letters *CNN* over her left breast.

The camerawoman adjusts the focus ring on her camera, using the words on the podium, *President of the United States*, to sharpen the focus on the camera's 4" LCD screen.

The man mimics her action using his 3" display. "Hey, can you guys use another camera person? It's so tough out there."

"How did you get in here, anyway?" she says, squinting her eyes.

The man blows on his coffee. He takes another sip, but it still burns his lips.

A man in a black suit steps out from a side door and walks onto the stage. The people sit up. The chatter stops. A reporter in the audience writes, "Press secretary arrives first." The reporter behind him writes, "*Secretario de Prensa entra primero.*" Another reporter in front writes, "*Naunang dumating ang punong tagapagsalita.*"

The press secretary addresses the crowd, "Thank you all for coming. The president will be out momentarily. He will give a brief speech, and then have only limited time to answer questions."

Two men in black suits step out from the door, touching the earpieces in their ears. Then the man of the moment comes out.

Camera clicks fill the room.

The curvaceous camerawoman checks her viewfinder as the president stands at the podium. She pulls out slightly, ensuring the president's gray hair is near the top of the frame. His blue tie and green eyes pop on the screen. The high-definition sensor captures the glimmer in his American flag lapel pin.

The skinny cameraman bumps the leg on his tripod. He tries to steady the camera, but his shoe hits the cup, nearly dumping the scalding coffee.

The president stares at the crowd. He takes a deep breath and lets it out slowly through his lips. He opens his mouth, a fragment of a word emerging, but then he shakes his head, the wrinkles in his forehead deepening.

"My people have prepared a speech, but I don't want to start with that. I want to start by saying that I am deeply sorry for what has happened. My heart and the heart of the first lady go out to the families of the victims. I will do everything in my power to find who is behind this attack." He squeezes his hand into a fist. "America is strong. America is a leader. America will not be terrorized by a minority of individuals who rely on cowardly acts. I've been president for over five years now, and I know this past election has been very partisan with the environmental debates and economic issues, but let me make this very clear. The defense of this great nation supersedes all of these issues. I plan to ensure our generation, our kids' generation, and their kids' generation will have a safe country and a safe planet to live in. I want to open up for questions now."

A switch flips as everyone's hand rises. The president nods at a blonde woman in the second row.

"Mr. President, some say that these recent attacks occurred because of your focus on the environment. Many scientists are extremely concerned about Global Warming. Reports out of Germany suggest a major catastrophe is imminent. Earth is doomed. How do you respond?"

The president puts his right elbow on the podium and leans in. "Now I want to make myself crystal clear. *Justice* is my top priority. And once the hardworking and skilled individuals in my departments bring justice to the victims of this attack and their families, I plan to do everything in my power to ensure the safety of all Americans."

He looks up. More hands rise.

The curvaceous camerawoman takes off her shoe. The skinny cameraman narrows his eyes.

Two men in suits charge toward her.

A wire falls out of the shoe. She goes to throw it, but the skinny cameraman douses her with his coffee, scalding her face and eyes.

Shrieks erupt. Two men in suits shield the president as four more swarm the crowd.

"Everyone stay seated!" a tall man shouts, his gun drawn.

Three men hold the camerawoman down. More suited men grab the president. "Wait! Wait!" he yells.

The reporters simmer down and look at the president.

He widens his eyes. "Do you really care about Global Warming?"

1

A withered coffee cup hides under the shell of a parked car. A breeze blows it into the light where it ignites into a fireball, sending a cloud of heat into the air.

Burned-out shells of cars line the road. Rubble fills a street. Exposed blacktop on another road radiates heat. Scraps of metal are a memory of a skyscraper. The blue sky has turned orange, the sun now a fireball.

Three creatures walk through the furnace, slowly, cautiously, three mice on the lookout for the cat. They wear tan suits, hardened, heavily insulated, cooled with dry ice. The suits could come from the closet of an astronaut or of a scientist specializing in the study of pestilence. Glass visors across their helmets shield their eyes, visors engineered to let in no more than 5% of light. The three scientists carry hetoscopes with probes that measure and track temperature change, accurate to within 1/1000 of a degree Fahrenheit.

The scientist in the back stops at the smoldering coffee cup. She is twenty-five, a freshman scientist, the first time she has ever been to the surface. Her glove touches the cup, which breaks apart into ash, floating away into the heat.

"Come on. Let's keep moving," the senior scientist's voice echoes inside her helmet.

She looks at him, ten feet in front near a piece of mangled metal. He waves her forward.

"This is amazing how fast the heat burns down to the molecular level," she says.

"We'll also be burned up if we stop to smell the roses," he says.

"Our suits have been vetted through R and D, but they're not burn proof," the third middle-aged female scientist says.

The freshman scientist hustles to reach the other two. They all turn down another street.

A four-inch metal spoon is lying on the road. A dozen American coins are hiding under the metal of a car. The freshman scientist stoops down to examine them. The date on one is 2019.

"The year I was born," she says.

"Do you remember when the earthquake hit?" the senior scientist asks.

"I wasn't even one. I don't even remember the surface."

"So this really *is* your first time up here," he says.

"Yes, it is, sir."

He twitches his nose. "They keep sending me younger and younger ones."

"You're just getting older and older," the middle-aged scientist says.

He chuckles.

"Do you remember, sir?" the freshman scientist asks.

He grabs some coins and starts stacking them. "I was thirty-four. I just got promoted to Associate Professor at Penn in Computer Science. I was engaged; my wedding was a month away."

"What happened, sir?" the freshman scientist asks.

"Boom!" He knocks over the stacked coins. "It hit at nine in the morning that day. July second, twenty twenty. It was chaos. Millions of people died, just like that."

"What about your fiancée, sir?" she asks.

He pauses, a cloud of sadness forming in his eyes.

"Levels out here are twenty degrees higher than last month," the middle-aged scientist says.

The senior scientist clears his throat. "It must be a glitch. That's impossible based on our projections."

The freshman scientist gestures to a metallic object half-buried in rubble. "What is *that*, sir?"

"The Liberty Bell," he says.

She walks toward it. "I've only read about it. It's still holding up."

The middle-aged scientist shakes her head at her older colleague.

The senior scientist presses a button so that his radio only communicates with her. "Let her have this moment."

As the freshman scientist approaches the rubble, she sees the crack inside the Bell. She steps over a scorched wheelchair and crutches. The sun bounces off the Bell and sends a filtered glimmer into her eyes, which makes her smile.

She goes closer. IV poles, wheelchairs, and other metal pile around the Bell. She yanks up a set of crutches. Underneath, three human skulls glare back at her.

She clamors back, ready to fall, but the senior scientist catches her.

"Let's do our job," he says.

She nods and sees the middle-aged scientist already down the street.

The group reaches a bank of four turbines, spinning at thousands of revolutions per minute. A shield of twelve-inch thick metal blocks the direct sun. The sound of the intense spinning penetrates the scientists' suits.

The middle-aged scientist removes a hose from her hetoscope and hands it to the senior scientist. He plugs it into his pack.

The freshman scientist stares at the rotating blades on one of the turbines. She smells the scent of heat—the same scent that creeps through the common areas setting off alarms, the same scent that finds its way through the feet of bedrock and into her bedroom, the same scent that leads to death. Beads of sweat form on her forehead.

"Come on!" the middle-aged scientist shouts.

"What's wrong?" the senior scientist says.

The freshman scientist takes a deep breath. "I feel hot."

"These suits can handle the heat for at least the next ten years," the senior scientist says.

"Hook your pack up and we'll get this done and be back underground," the middle-aged scientist says.

The freshman scientist hooks her hetoscope into the others as the middle-aged scientist plugs a cord into a control unit on the turbines. She flips a switch and slides a dial. "Something's wrong with this."

The senior scientist checks the connections.

A movement twenty yards away catches the attention of the freshman scientist. Underneath a scorched tractor-trailer is a Coca-

Cola sign on top of crumbled concrete. The sign still shows a hint of red.

The freshman scientist walks toward it. The sign moves slightly.

"Coca-Cola?" she says.

As she approaches, something moves under the sign.

She stops.

The sign remains still. She moves forward and sees eyes blink on a face. Sweat pours down her face. She's six feet away from the remains of the sign when she makes out the body of a man, naked, skin blistered. He points up at the sky and mouths something.

The freshman scientist jumps back.

"No! Rachel!" the senior scientist shouts.

She loses her balance on a stone and falls back. The edge of a piece of metal punctures her suit as flames engulf her.

The other scientists reach her as she flails her arms in a panic. Inside her suit, blood starts dripping from her nose. She sees the fireball through her shield so she presses buttons on the suit.

A buzzer blasts.

The senior scientist sprays thick white foam from an extinguisher, but he misses her suit.

She presses more buttons. The suit opens and falls off her body. She runs through the heat, as her body ignites into flames.

The middle-aged scientist uses her extinguisher, but the flames only intensify.

The freshman scientist bounces off the frame of a car and drops down, the fire consuming her.

The senior scientist reaches her body, but the fire is too intense. The only thing he can make out is the American flag on the shoulder of her suit, but the fire quickly devours it.

2

Coffee pours into a coffee cup. James Wilson sips the concoction as he stands in a room the size of a closet. A clock hangs on the wall showing "7:35." Underneath it on the concrete is a picture of a palm tree on a beach. A card table and three chairs sit against the corner. A combination lock protects a box the size of a microwave and next to it is a five-gallon jug of water that says, "Week 5, 2045."

James is thirty-five years old with pale white skin and full black hair, a messy part down the middle. A blue jumpsuit covers him with tar marking the shoulders and back. UVASHIELD is written on the label over the left side of his chest.

His nine-year-old son, Brian, runs in wearing goggles and shooting a plastic gun.

"Hey, I told you not to play with Dad's stuff," James says, grabbing the goggles.

"I'm sorry, Dad," Brian replies.

"Do you know how many credits that cost me? If you break them, I won't be able to afford your school. And you like your school, right?"

He nods his head. "It's just that they're so cool. It makes everything look big."

James smiles. "They *are* cool. It helps me see when I work near the surface."

"Why is mom still sleeping?" Brian asks.

"Well, she worked late last night, tiger."

"I'm up now with all this talking," Brian's mom says. Her name is Janice. She is thin with skin as pale as the model in a vampire movie, but her eyes are blue and unforgettable.

"Oh, I'm sorry, honey," James says.

She kisses him. "It's okay. I don't want my two guys starting their day on an empty stomach." Janice pulls out the chair for her son.

He sits down and starts reading a comic book.

"How was the ward?" James asks as she grabs three meal packs from the cupboard.

"Bad." She shakes her head. "The long-term effect of sun deprivation does terrible things to the body."

Both parents look at their son as he scratches the pale skin on his forearm.

Suddenly, the lights turn off.

"Mom!" Brian shouts.

"I'm right here, baby," she says.

"Come on, guys," James says. "Stop playing around."

The lights pop back on.

James exhales. "The crews we have don't know what they're doing."

"Why can't we get out of this quadrant?" Janice says. "This place is smaller than our last one."

"Our last home is probably on fire now with the shields failing in that quadrant. You're lucky we got out."

"Well, we're lucky that our son is going to Harvard," she says, placing a wafer on a plate in front of Brian.

"I'm working a double today," James says.

"I got a shift too." She hands him a plate with the same type of wafer on it.

He kisses her.

"Our son is the ticket out of here," Janice whispers into her husband's ear.

The lights flicker. A buzzer rings in James' pocket. He pulls out a walkie-talkie and answers it. "Yeah."

"We're getting heavy surges," the voice says.

"I know. We're seeing it now in quadrant six," James says, looking at the lights.

"We need you at turbines two and four A in quadrant four. Meet your crew there," the voice says.

James looks into his wife's blue eyes, and for a moment, they're no longer blue; they're gray. "I'm on my way," he replies.

James gives her a peck on the cheek and rubs his son's head. "See you guys later," he says on his way to the door.

"Wait, your breakfast!" Janice shouts.

"I'll get something on the way," he says, shutting the door.

"Mom?" Brian goes.

She puts her arms around him. "Yes, baby."

"How come Alex gets to eat real meat?"

"You know how his parents have good jobs."

"Do you have a good job?"

"Your dad and I work hard. But if you study hard, one day you'll have the whole world." She stares at the picture of the beautiful beach, the sun shining brightly.

3

Palm trees filter the sun as it shines brightly in the blue sky. A pigeon perches on a branch and sings.

Alex Mercer sits on his couch, staring at the bird through the window in the ceiling of his home. He's nine years old with a healthy tan and a healthy smile. Next to him on the couch is a ten-inch smart tablet showing a yellow taxicab on the page of a comic book.

The bird squawks.

Alex gets up and stands on the couch. He reaches for the glass ceiling. He's only two feet away from the bird. It's right there, its white feathers, its yellow beak, its tiny nails.

"Alex!" his mom says. "You're going to fall and hurt yourself. What are you doing?"

"We're learning about birds in school."

His mom is Melissa Mercer, engineer, chief executive officer, wife, and mother of one. She is six feet tall with long slender legs, supple and soft. She has shoulder-length brown hair and tanned skin that complements her navy business jacket and skirt.

Alex falls onto the couch and into a remote control. The image through the ceiling changes to outer space.

"See," Melissa says. "You're going to break it."

Alex hits a button. The image goes black, and then the screen retracts, as the color orange filters into the room, the sun igniting the sky into a storm of fire.

"What happens if that glass cracks, Mom?" Alex asks.

"It won't crack," she says as she applies moisturizer to her face.

"If it cracks, we're dead," Alex's father says.

"Richard, stop," Melissa says.

Richard Mercer walks in wearing a Penn State T-shirt and shorts. He has a trimmed beard and thick glasses and he's holding a book titled, *American Films of the 2010s.*

"I'm sorry," Richard says. "What's gotten into you the past few days?"

"Nothing," Melissa replies. "It's just that you're going to scare him. Don't talk like that." She sees Richard scratching the back of his head. "What's wrong?"

"I just had this weird dream."

"Really?" Melissa says, staring at the taxicab on Alex's smart tablet.

"Are you having dreams too?" Richard asks.

She remains fixated on the yellow in the cab, yellow so bright and so bold that it makes her stop breathing.

Alex jumps up, bringing her back to reality. "Mom, I know all about the surface. We're learning about it in school. I know that if the sun hits our skin, it will burn it off."

"Hey, I thought you were learning about the birds," Melissa says.

"He'll be fine." Richard kisses her.

"Make sure you eat breakfast. I can't find my watch." Melissa searches through a drawer. A twinge in her head causes her to stop and rub her temples.

"Make sure *you* eat breakfast," Richard says, grabbing the watch from the couch and handing it to her.

She smiles and kisses him.

"I already made you something," he says. "Come eat, Alex, with your mom."

Richard leads the way past a tanning bed device labeled "Sim-Sun" and into a room the size of a bedroom. There's a full-size refrigerator, microwave, and electric stove. On the table are crisped bacon, toast, jelly, and orange juice alongside three empty plates.

"What's with the royal treatment?" Melissa says.

"No classes. I only have office hours today," he replies.

Alex hits a button on the wall. The ceiling opens up showing the burning sun, which fills the room with the color orange.

"Alex, do we have to see this now?" Melissa says.

"Why hide the truth?" Richard puts toast and bacon onto the three plates.

"Do we have to discuss this now? I thought we were eating breakfast. Put that nice beach scene back on."

Alex goes to the control panel on the wall and presses some more buttons. A screen slides across the ceiling. An outer space scene changes to a rollercoaster ride.

"Stop playing," Melissa says.

The scene changes to the blue sky, the sun shining brightly, the breeze dancing with the palm trees. The pigeon sits on the branch and chirps loudly. The Mercer family stares at the bird as it looks at them and sings. Another bird perches on the branch. Both sing together.

Suddenly, the lights cut out as darkness surrounds them.

"Mom?" Alex shouts.

"I'm right here," Melissa says through the darkness.

"Did you forget to pay the power bill?" Richard says.

The lights come back, the scene above distorted, the birds split in half revealing the digital facade.

"This isn't funny," Melissa says.

A *ding-dong* filters through the home.

Alex runs to the wall. "I'll get it."

"No, let Dad get it," Melissa says.

Richard walks to the wall and flips a switch. On the eight-inch screen, a military man with camouflaged fatigues stares at him.

"May I help you?" Richard says.

"Mrs. Mercer, please," he goes.

Richard shrugs. "No good morning?"

Melissa goes to the screen.

"Good morning, ma'am," the military man says. "The eagle requires your attention."

"Is this related to the blackout? We've never had a blackout hit our quadrant."

"We cannot discuss classified information here, Mrs. Mercer."

"I'm with my family," she says.

More ringing comes from the kitchen table.

"You have three minutes, Mrs. Mercer. This is an urgent matter."

"I'll be right out," she says, turning off the wall panel.

"The phone," Alex shouts over the ringing. "I'll get it."

"No, *I'll* get it," Melissa says.

"What's going on?" Richard asks.

She shrugs, and then answers the phone.

"Mrs. Mercer, there are some major issues happening," a male voice says.

"I know. The military is at my front door."

"I'm watching them at your front door, ma'am. I have our chopper. Our blue teams are dispatched. I have some raw data here you need to see."

"I'm walking out of my house now." Melissa ends the call. She puts some papers in a briefcase and fixes her suit.

"Your breakfast," Richard says as she leaves the kitchen. He gives her a piece of dark toast. "Sorry, it's burned," he says.

Melissa stops dead, staring at the toast. She looks at her son and her husband.

"What's wrong, Mom?"

She kneels down and looks into her son's eyes. "You have a good day at school today. Ask your teacher about the different types of birds. You'll love the blue birds. They're beautiful."

Alex smiles. She kisses him.

Melissa stands up and kisses her husband, Alex holding her waist. She receives a text message on her smart phone, "Data is correct!!!"

Melissa stops. Her husband's lips don't faze her.

"What data is correct?" he asks.

She remains frozen.

"I know I'm not supposed to ask about some of your work."

Melissa remains detached, her eyes staring at the toast, the black marks dark, deep, a cancer.

"Hey!" Richard says. Melissa comes out of her trance. He leans toward her ear and whispers, "Whatever it is, your family loves you."

She looks into his eyes and swallows hard. "I love you both," she says, embracing her family.

The doorbell sounds again. She takes a bite out of the toast.

4

A woman in a red dress, breasts bulging, skirt hiked up, loiters at a train stop, holding a stack of marketing postcards that say, "1 Credit off S-Beer with this Card."

The air is thick, the stench of body odor clinging to the humidity.

A train screams to a halt. The doors burst open and hundreds of people pour out. Some wear dress slacks and shirts, while others wear navy work suits or lab coats labeled with UVASHIELD.

The woman in the red dress offers the cards to the crowd.

In the mass, James fights to exit the train.

A tremor shakes the platform. Some people shout. Some people cheer.

James grabs a handle, but a chubby guy wearing a torn sweatshirt bumps into him. Other people push to exit. James struggles, but breaks free from the train.

He bumps into the woman in the red dress, knocking her to the ground. A panel opens on the back of her head and wires fall out. James stuffs them back in and tries to reattach the back-plate.

"The wife not giving you any lately?" a burly voice says.

Standing over James is a chubby Samoan man with short gray hair and wrinkles as deep as his voice. He sports a handlebar mustache curled like curlicues. His name is Chop.

"Don't just stand there," James says. "Help me here."

As he finishes screwing on her head plate, Chop grabs her breasts and looks into her eyes.

"They're making these things even more real now," Chop says.

A woman in a work suit sees the two guys on the ground and shakes her head.

"Hey, she said she was into threesomes," Chop goes.

James finishes fixing her head. "Help me lift her up." He grabs under her arms as Chop grabs her breasts.

"One, two, *three*." They lift her back on her feet.

She starts handing out cards again as if nothing happened.

"We could have some fun with this one," Chop says.

Another tremor shakes the area. The woman in the red dress falls over again.

"Either she had too much to drink, or this place is shaking," Chop says.

James shakes his head. "Let's go. We've got work to do."

Both men walk into the open area. Thousands of people roam. The place looks like a New York City subway station with ceilings that reach three hundred feet into the air. Above the crowd, large flat-screen monitors show the globe spinning with the message, "Have you been vaccinated against Hepatitis T?" Vendors sell wafers with signs that read, "Tastes like chicken! – Only 10 Credits." Smoke billows from vents. Twenty scooters line the outside of a shop. A man sells goggles from a blanket. A woman covered in scars holds her hand out.

"Talk about a dirty-ass quadrant," James says.

"Why the hell do we even have to fix this?" Chop says. "Let 'em all burn."

"Hey, we're all in this together."

Three rats scurry across Chop's feet. He punts one into a sign reading "Healthy Food."

"We're in a ticking time bomb, brother. Wake up! Would you choose saving these punks over your wife, your kid?"

A man covered with dirt confronts them. "Food, sir. Please."

James flicks off the man and pushes Chop forward. "We have work to do."

A few steps outside of Chop's view, James drops a saltine-size packet on the ground. The hungry man lunges for it. "Thank you."

James and Chop snake through the crowd. The sound of an engine overwhelms them. As they move, their pores cry, the humidity thickening, the heat heightening.

When they turn the corner, the smell of sewage attacks them. Both men wince, and then continue toward a ventilation system larger than a group of jet engines.

Two of the turbines are running, their thirty-foot blades rotating. Another man in a blue uniform is on a catwalk near one of the immobile turbines, its blades an awaiting guillotine.

"Didn't we fix this last month?" Chop says.

"Nice of you to join us, ladies," a beefy black man wearing a hard hat shouts over the noise. He's the brute of the crew. His name is Reeko.

He gives James and Chop hats.

"Must be the voltage regulators from the heat," James yells over the cry of the turbines.

"That's your area, man," Reeko says. "Fix it this time."

"I've patched just about everything I can," James says.

"The boss wants us to fix it or the people in this quadrant might as well be burnt toast. I'll let you tell them that."

Chop gives James heavy eyes.

They climb a ladder on the wall and head toward the turbines.

"This reminds me of the time in Vegas," Chop says.

"Vegas? Sin City, right?" James says.

"When you were in diapers, I was a working man out there for two years. I used to work for the arena. We'd show all the big events, boxing matches, concerts, NCAA tournaments."

"What does this have to do with the turbines?" James says as both of them make their way to join the other man.

"What?" Chop shouts through the noise.

"It's too loud. Tell me this story later," James says.

"Look who decided to wake up," a skinny guy shouts. His name is Bones, cocked and ready to fire.

James checks inside an access panel with a flashlight.

"I had to leave the honey in my bed to join this circle jerk?" Chop shouts.

"I'm sure her rubber skin and wires won't miss you," Bones replies.

James stands up and wipes the sweat from his brow.

"What's the diagnosis, Doctor?" Bones says.

James shakes his head and exhales.

"Come on, brother," Chop says. "You can fix it."

"The voltage regulator is gone," James shouts.

"There's a backup," Chop replies.

"It's fried too. Uh, you two guys remove the backup from number one," James says to Bones and Reeko as he gestures to one of the moving turbines. "We'll have to use that one as the primary here."

"What about four?" Reeko asks, looking at the second immobile turbine.

"Let's get this one going first."

James grabs a long screwdriver and starts rewiring the circuit.

Two helicopters approach the men. One is aggressive, painted in camouflage with its pilot and co-pilot wearing the same color. The other is white with UVASHIELD marked on its side. Inside, the pilot maneuvers the chopper to allow Melissa and her assistant to observe.

"Smile, boys," Reeko says. "The big boss wants to say hi."

Chop smiles, waves at her, and gives her the thumbs up. "I'd bang her."

James locks eyes with Melissa and explains the grimness of their situation, of their world, of their lives, in his somber stare.

5

A bead of sweat forms on the back of Melissa's neck. It slides down her back, tickling her senses. She tries to reach around to scratch, but the cabin of the chopper is too confined, so she accepts the itch.

"The drones," Melissa's assistant says. His name is Philip, a man who knows how to make a Full Windsor knot on his tie in the morning, only to loosen it by lunch.

"Philip, these technicians are keeping us alive down here," Melissa says. She locks eyes with James.

"They're so filthy, Mrs. Mercer. Oh, look at that skinny one."

"They will fix this," Melissa says, nodding at James, who nods back.

The pilot's voice in the military chopper cuts in on their headsets, "We must go, ma'am. The president is waiting."

"I just needed to get a visual of the damage." She swallows and twirls her finger at her pilot.

The military helicopter leads the way above the mess. Men throw stones at the choppers. Others scream and throw their hands in the air. More trains zip through the tunnels.

Inside the chopper, Melissa watches the stones and trash hitting the window. Behind her is the third man inside the helicopter, a man who tried his hand at nearly all of the positions offered at UVASHIELD. He is a two-finger typer, failing the computer exam he took. But the keyboard he uses now only has one key—the trigger. His name is Lance and he grips his pistol tighter as the projectiles hit the glass.

Melissa sees a scrawny guy licking a piece of rubber. He wears no shirt, the tattoo of a skull on his back, the ribs in his body showing.

"Ma'am, please sit back, away from the glass," Lance says.

She leans back, fixing her collar, and stares at the spinning blades of a turbine.

"Would it be that bad to get rid of the excess?" Philip says, looking at the mob of people beneath him.

"I'm not paying you for opinions," Melissa says.

"I'm sorry, ma'am."

The choppers fly over the trains and arrive at a concrete wall with a bay door. Above is a sign that says, "To Quadrant 3."

The choppers wait at the door as it opens slowly. Past the door, a long catacomb of passageways offers a maze. The choppers speed down a corridor, and then turn down another. After thirty seconds, a large sign appears, "Entering the New White House. All communication devices must be turned off."

Men in camouflage clutch rifles and walk catwalks above two turrets defending another massive bay door. Below the catwalks is a control room protected by bulletproof glass. Men and women manage the controls inside the station. Some wear headsets, while others monitor video surveillance feeds.

The helicopters hover in front of the bay door.

"We have Mrs. Melissa Mercer, CEO of UVASHIELD, here for the president," the pilot in the military chopper says into his headset radio as he looks at the man inside the control room.

"Affirmative. UVASHIELD, please take bay twelve." The man presses a button on the panel. The door opens.

Lance bites his lip and stares at the military men.

Melissa receives a text message on her smart tablet. It reads, "Honey, Alex has a PTA meeting tonight. Can you make it?" She replies, "If I make it out of this meeting alive. Talk soon."

"Please disable all communication devices," the voice of the man in the control room says on the radio.

Melissa disables the signal on her smart tablet, and then looks at Philip.

"I'm offline, ma'am," he says, fumbling with his smart tablet.

Melissa glances at Lance.

"Mine stays on," he says.

Dozens of choppers line the deck. Some are the identical military model escorting Melissa. Others are smaller choppers with room only for one. The place looks like the top of a destroyer ship, but instead of the open blue sky, a concrete roof seals the area one thousand feet up. In the middle, four fifty-foot-wide turbines similar to those in quadrant 4 rotate and fill the area with noise.

The military chopper guides Melissa to the empty bay marked, "12." Four men in fatigues stand guard as well as a clean-shaven man in a business suit wearing glasses. His name is Ross and he's the president's chief of staff.

When the chopper lands, Ross opens the door and helps Melissa out. "Mrs. Mercer, you're late."

"I had to collect some data."

"Right this way," he says ushering her toward a twenty-foot American flag flapping from the wind swirling in the bay.

Lance goes to follow.

"No," Ross says. "Your security guard must stay."

Lance grips his gun. "I'm not a fuckin' rent-a-cop."

Two military men approach.

"It's okay," Melissa says, nodding at Lance, who stays back at the chopper.

Ross leads the way. Philip follows, holding two briefcases. He smiles at Ross, who presses his lips together.

Two army men guard a door. Overhead is a sign that says, "The Office of the President of the United States of America." Melissa enters as a sterile hallway reaches for a mile with florescent bulbs shining, the same bulbs from a hospital wing. The walls are white with a mural of the White House in Washington D.C. painted on one of them.

"Do you have all your data?" Ross asks.

Melissa looks at Philip. He nods.

"We're ready," Melissa replies.

Down a hallway, suits, fatigues, and lab coats flurry. The temperature is cool. Melissa takes a deep breath as the smell of coconuts surrounds her.

"Do you smell that?" Philip asks.

"It's wonderful," she replies, grinning.

They turn the corner and behold a conference room. Above the door, a seal showing the bald eagle proudly displays with the label, "Executive Office of the President of the United States."

They enter as the smell of coconuts vanishes, replaced by the stench of sweat. Inside, four sixty-inch flat-screen monitors are showing the same seal of the president. A conference table is in the center of the room with four people in business suits already seated. At the head of the table with a view of the entire room is an empty seat, a plaque labeled, "President of the United States."

A smaller plaque is next to it labeled, "Secretary of Defense." Sitting behind it is a middle-aged man with an air of arrogance. His friends call him pudgy; his enemies call him fat, and he doesn't have many friends. He is Secretary of Defense Robert Dunner. As Melissa enters, he glares at her.

Melissa sits across from him behind a hand-written nametag showing, "Melissa Mercer, CEO – UVASHIELD." Philip sits down behind her and hands her some papers and a smart tablet from one of the briefcases.

"The President of the United States," a woman announces from the door at the side.

Everyone stands up. A tall man walks out with salt-and-pepper hair parted to the side. He is Jonathan H. Brooks, a self-aware man in his sixties.

He nods at Melissa before sitting down. "Let's get started."

Everyone sits down except for Ross. He clicks a button. The screens in the room display, "Daily Presidential Briefing – July 17, 2045." The screen changes to a map of Philadelphia, Baltimore, and Washington D.C. and the underground city that connects them. One screen shows, "U.S. population: 99,783 – World population: Unknown."

Ross clears his throat. "Scientists have not been able to pick up any external signals. There was an accident yesterday during a routine status check of the shields."

A video montage shows the three scientists combing the surface. They hook their hetoscopes into the shield over the turbines. The video becomes shaky as the freshman scientist panics. She rips off her suit as the other two scientists spray their extinguishers. Then she erupts into flames.

Gasps fill the room. Melissa swallows hard and rubs her temples.

The video stops on the freshman scientist engulfed in flames. Beyond her, the eyes of the scorched man under the tractor-trailer shine and cause everyone in the room to look away, except for Secretary Dunner.

"What is that?" Secretary Dunner says.

"Just a reflection," Ross replies.

"A reflection? That's a fuckin'…creature."

Ross moves the video forward a frame. The fire distorts the eyes of the man.

"Turn that off," the president says.

Ross switches the screens to a black image.

"We've been underground twenty years now. How the hell is something living up there?" Secretary Dunner says.

"Let's not get off topic," President Brooks says. "What happened to this poor young scientist?"

"Faulty suit," Secretary Dunner goes.

The room looks at Melissa.

"Sir, I can assure you that our suits are able to withstand external temperatures up to two hundred degrees Fahrenheit," Melissa says.

The president looks at a young man in a lab coat seated at the table. "Two hundred degrees buys us how much time?" the president asks.

"Based on our trending data, ten years," the young man replies.

"Your damn suit killed this woman. We should try her for murder," Secretary Dunner says.

President Brooks raises his hand. "Okay, that's enough."

"Sir, I have some new data here. This, uh, can explain this incident," Melissa says.

"I think we've heard enough from you," Secretary Dunner says.

The president shoots his eyes at Secretary Dunner. "Let her talk."

"Sir, we've prepared a brief slide presentation," Melissa says. Philip hands her a flash drive, which she gives to Ross.

"May I?" she asks, standing. The president nods.

The image on the screen shows a map of Philadelphia, Baltimore, and Washington D.C.

"As you know, part of our company's mission is to manage the turbine ventilation systems that purify the air. These systems provide a safe, clean breathing environment for America. We have turbines across the six active quadrants that span the borders of our underground nation."

On screen, the image shows three-dozen dots spread across the map.

"In order for these turbines to work properly, special steel shields on the surface deflect the direct radiation from the sun into their air handlers."

"We know all this, Mrs. Mercer," Secretary Dunner says. "What does this have to do with the suit?"

"Each ventilation system has temperature monitors that collect raw temperature data. Our research scientists noticed something strange over the past few weeks. We thought it was just random spikes in temperatures we've seen over the years. But then we realized that after these spikes occurred, the temperature maintained a higher level than before. When the three-person crew from your department went out yesterday to collect data, they walked right into one of these flares. Temperatures were not one sixty, but over two hundred, which is beyond the capacity of our suits."

On screen, a chart of temperature data displays.

"So we have random temperature flares and we're gaining a few degrees," Secretary Dunner says. "What does this matter? Are you a liberal, Mrs. Mercer?"

"The temperature increase starts at just a few degrees as we are seeing, but the rate is not following a linear curve; it's following an exponential curve."

"What does this mean?" the president asks.

"Sir, based on our model, temperatures will exceed the capacity of our shields not in ten years as we originally predicted."

"She's lying," Secretary Dunner says. "She's just a business-woman scaring us to give her more money."

"Sir, I wish money would solve this," she says.

The president looks at his scientists at the conference table. "What data are you seeing?"

The woman in the lab coat starts thumbing through charts as another man behind her whispers into her ear. They both squint their eyes, and then the woman says, "How did we miss this? I see it now. We must verify the data. But Mrs. Mercer looks to be correct. We need to share our data between her company and our department."

"Hold on a second," Secretary Dunner says. "Sharing classified information with an outside entity is a matter of national security. She's just trying to grow her company. Where did your scientists get their degrees, Mrs. Mercer? Fire State University?"

"Stop!" President Brooks shouts.

Everyone freezes.

"Let's cut out the pissing contest here, Bob," the president says. He turns to Melissa. "Let's assume you're correct as I know that after this meeting, we're going to have every scientist with a security clearance left in America, left on this whole planet, analyzing this. So what are we looking at here?"

Everyone in the room looks at Melissa.

She swallows and clicks the slide. "Seven days," she reads from the screen.

"Hogwash!" Secretary Dunner says.

"Seven days until what?" the president asks.

The next slide shows an animation of the map. Fire icons replace the turbines, and then the animation changes to a fire over the entire nation.

Gasps come from some of the audience members.

"I'm not going to let this woman stand here and feed us this shit. How much money do you want?" Secretary Dunner continues.

"Sir, I wish I had different news. I wish I could throw money at this problem, but this is bad—very, *very* bad. Our turbine systems are running on their last legs. This morning on my way here, I saw two turbines in quadrant four that are non-operational, causing breathing problems and rolling blackouts last night. We have the best engineers and technicians working for us, but this is something that I can't yet provide a handle on."

The president stands up. Everyone goes to stand. "No, sit," he says as everyone sits down, including Melissa. "First of all, none of this leaves this room, *none of this*. I remind you of your security clearances." He looks at Security Dunner. The president walks around to the center of the room. "I've been president of what's left of America for seven years now. I've seen the population go from two hundred thousand down to now under a hundred thousand. I've seen poverty, death, riots. But beyond all this mess, I think of my family, my kids. My daughter is sixteen years old. And she has never seen the sun, except through a three-foot-thick filter. She needs to take pills to keep her eyes from crossing, and she lies in a box to keep her skin from turning pale. She has never seen a sunset, never seen the birds flying in the blue sky above the beach. Everyone younger than twenty years old falls into my daughter's category." He looks around him. "Everyone in this room has experienced the world above us, the world before the earthquakes and the fireballs. I knew this day would come, when time catches up to us. Whether it was ten years, or ten days, I knew this day would come when we would have to make a decision. Maybe we should just let the human race expire. I ask myself, what are we doing down here? Why are we hiding from the inevitable? But we're all human, and humans have such a passion for life and for living. I want us to take this moment to think about our families, think about our children. And then, let's give it our *best* shot to find a solution to save them, to save the human race. Everyone has twenty-four hours to come up with a solution. Following your security clearances, I expect this to remain only in this room and with those with a strict need-to-know. You all have twenty-four hours to save the human race."

Everyone stares at the fire icon on the screen.

6

A bald eagle soars in the sky above a mountain. It perches on a lone branch overlooking the vastness of the mountain.

"The bald eagle," the short and chubby teacher says. She stands at a podium next to the projector screen showing the video. "Does anyone know what the bald eagle symbolizes?"

She looks at the class of a dozen students. Alex and Brian sit next to each other, books open, pencils sharp.

"America," Alex says.

"That's right, Alex," the teacher says. "The bald eagle is the symbol of America."

The image of the projector flickers.

"Don't worry, kids."

"My dad will fix it," Brian says.

The image comes back.

"What's that, Brian?" the teacher asks.

"My dad is fixing the turbines. That's why the lights keep flickering."

"His dad is dirty," a blonde girl says in the front row. The other kids snicker, except for Alex.

"That's enough," the teacher says to the class. "Brian, your father has a very important job."

"Well, my dad is famous. He's on the news channel," the same girl says.

"I said that's enough," the teacher says. "Let's get back to our lesson. I'll have time to meet all your parents tonight."

"The bald eagle is a member of the Kingdom Animalia," she continues.

"Hey, are your parents coming tonight?" Brian whispers to Alex.

"I don't know. My mom's always working. How about yours?"

"My dad's always working too," Brian replies, picking up his pencil.

Through the tunnels five miles away, Brian's father picks up a screwdriver. He adjusts a blow-off valve inside the guts of turbine four. The other three turbines are spinning, blowing hot, sticky air around the men working.

Smoke swirls as Chop solders a cable.

Hanging from a safety harness, Bones lubricates the gears.

Reeko carries a fifty-pound control unit across the catwalk as sweat saturates the neck of his work suit. He sets the unit down in front of Chop. "Come on, ladies!"

Chop looks at him. "Go home to your mother."

"I'll make you a deal. If you ladies get this going, I'll buy the first round."

"I can't drink anymore of that simulated beer made out of hand sanitizer," Bones says, swinging back to the catwalk.

"No. The *real* stuff, a nice cold bottle of Miller," Reeko continues.

"Ya hear that, James," Chop says. "The *real* stuff."

"Why didn't you tell me that earlier?" James says.

"The boss wants this done," Reeko adds.

"Tell him to come down and help," James says, waving a screwdriver.

"No, not that boss, the boss' boss. The lady on top. Her assistant just radioed. Something big is brewing. She wants all available techs to get us to one hundred percent."

"One hundred percent! Ha!" Chop says. "The only time we've been at one hundred percent was when we went underground twenty years ago."

"She's watching us, ladies," Reeko says.

"Whoa! Whoa!" Bones yells from the catwalk as he dangles over the edge with his safety harness, three hundred feet above the concrete.

Chop runs over, reaches down, and then pulls him up.

"Come on, get your shit together," Reeko says.

James gets a vibration in his pocket. He pulls out his smart phone. "When are you coming home? We have Brian's open house."

James types, "Still working."

Ten miles through the catacombs, Melissa Mercer is sitting at her desk surrounded by papers. She's writing formulas onto a notepad with a pencil. A smart tablet is next to her showing a chart of numbers.

Melissa puts the pencil down and takes a deep breath, a twinge of staleness in the air. She stands up and glances at the diploma on the wall: "Melissa Mercer – Bachelor of Science – Mechanical Engineering – University of Pennsylvania – Class of 2020." She walks to the window of her office and stares at her staff.

Dozens of people in lab coats work. Some sit behind computers. Some make calculations on whiteboards. Others blow extinguishers on a fire suit.

A ring sounds from her phone on her desk. She sits back down and answers it.

"Hey. How's your day going?" Richard says.

"This is the worst day of my life."

"What's wrong? Where did they take you this morning?"

She stares at a picture on her desk. She and Richard are sitting on a couch, smiling, holding a baby, the family exuding life and love.

"Do you remember that time when Alex was born?" she asks.

"Of course. I think about that time every day."

"Do you remember what the nurse said? The one who handed Alex to me right after he entered our world."

"Of course I remember," Richard says.

"Do you think it was strange that she said that? I mean, the way she said it."

"But she was wrong. The doctor was wrong. They were *all* wrong. And Alex is here with us. We're together."

Melissa smiles.

A knock sounds at her door. Philip opens it and puts his head inside. "Sorry, Mrs. Mercer. The president's office wants you on a conference call."

"I have to run," Melissa says into the phone.

"Remember. Alex's open house is tonight."

She stares at the photo and doesn't respond.

"I'll just go as the single parent again," Richard continues.

"Honey, I love you," she says. "You know that."

Before Richard can respond, Melissa ends the phone call. She focuses on the notepad and starts writing, "MC + M – E."

"Mrs. Mercer?" Philip says.

"I heard you the first time, Philip."

"I'm sorry, ma'am." He opens the door. "May I come in for a moment?"

She circles the equation. "What is it?"

"Ma'am. I was wondering about my mother. She doesn't know what I really do here and I know that she is trustworthy."

Melissa looks up.

"Shut the door, Philip, and come here."

"Yes, ma'am," he says, walking to the desk.

"I know this is scary. But we've come so far. I started this company because I knew I'd find a way to make our lives better, to make them as close to what they used to be before all this tragedy."

"You've done so much, Mrs. Mercer. We're here because of you."

"You've been with me a long time, Philip. I trust you."

"And I trust you, ma'am. I trust that you will know what to do."

"Will I?" she says, biting the pencil.

7

A car races across a bridge. Blue water flows underneath. Trees reach for the sky on the sides of the riverbank. A bird perches on one of the suspension cables.

"Next up are two of our wonderful engineers of the class, Alex Mercer and Brian Wilson," the chubby teacher says.

Alex and Brian walk to the front of the class. Alex wears a dress shirt, his teeth glimmering when he smiles. Brian wears a sweater vest, his hair slicked to the side.

From their chairs, twenty parents and other kids clap for the boys.

"Go get 'em, son," Richard says, giving Alex the thumbs up.

"Yay, honey!" Janice shouts.

"Boys, tell us all about your science project," the teacher says.

Alex and Brian look into the audience as their smiles fade.

"Where's your dad?" Alex whispers.

"I don't know. What about your mom?"

Both boys share a glance that seems to last forever.

Miles through the catacombs, an old man with dirt coating the scars on his face, wearing gloves with the fingers exposed, hair a ratty mess, is standing under the turbines. He looks up at James and Chop, whose hands are deep within the guts of the inoperable turbine.

"God wants you to stop! This is not part of his plan!" the grubby old man shouts.

Chop glances over the edge and sees the man and other stragglers. "We got an audience now."

Reeko walks over. "The locals are getting restless. Come on, pussies."

"They're always restless," James says. He puts a module into the control box; it doesn't fit. James punches it in, over and over.

"Nice engineering work," Reeko goes.

"It's already broken," Chop says.

"Give it one quarter power!" James shouts to Bones, who adjusts a dial.

A surge of power causes the lights in the area to flicker. Screams and cheers pour from more onlookers.

"This is the devil's work! The end is near!" the grubby old man shouts.

"Too much!" James yells, his hand still inside.

"Are you crazy?" Reeko yells at James.

The turbine kicks on, rotating slowly.

"Okay, give it more juice! Just a little!"

Bones turns the dial slightly. Sparks fly out of the control box and shower over James. He shouts and winces.

"When I say *now*, you turn it to one hundred percent," James says, grabbing a screwdriver. He bends the edge of the module to make better contact, straining to use all of his power.

Reeko and Chop stand back, eyes wide open.

"Now!" James gives it one more push; a voltage spike punches his body back.

The turbine kicks into high gear and starts rotating.

"I don't believe it!" Bones says.

James is hanging off the side of the catwalk without a harness.

Chop and Reeko run to him. "Give me your hand!" Chop shouts.

James lets one hand go, his body ready to fall, but Chop reaches over and yanks him up. James rolls onto the catwalk and takes a deep breath. "I owe you one."

"You scared the shit out of me," Chop says, shaking his head. "But you fixed it, brother."

"If I could give you a medal, I would," Reeko says. "You're one dedicated son of a bitch. Are you okay?"

"Never better," he says, wiping the grease onto his work uniform. "I'm just doing my job, giving these people the clean air they deserve."

"I could've done that," Bones says.

"Level-two techs are just here for clean up," Chop says.

"How long we got with this fix?" Reeko asks.

"Hopefully until we get new parts from corporate."

Chop laughs.

James checks his phone. It says, "Three Missed Calls." There is one text message that reads, "Going to Brian's event. Come if you can. He misses you."

"Let's get that drink, ladies. I'm a man of my word," Reeko says.

James starts cleaning up his pack.

"Let's go to the Ice Bar," Reeko adds, patting James on the back.

"Rain check," James says.

"Don't puss out on us," Bones goes.

"Family stuff."

"James and his family," Bones says.

"Let the bastard go," Reeko says. "He earned it."

Chop pats him on the back. "Nice work, brother. Tell Janice and Brian I said hi."

Through the dark corridors and stale air, Melissa is sitting at her desk, looking at numbers on her smart tablet.

A knock sounds at the door, but she keeps staring at her work.

Philip peeks inside. "Our techs got all the turbines in quadrant four back to one hundred percent operational."

"Does it really matter now?" she says.

Philip opens the door wider. "Ma'am, may I?"

She keeps her eyes on the smart tablet. "Can't you see I'm busy?"

Philip bites his lip and leaves.

The sound of silence engulfs her when the door shuts. She sits back and stares at a bug crawling on the ceiling. It moves slowly, its tentacles prodding the white walls. It has no fear, no desires, no conscience. The bug simply moves on instinct. Does it know about the world above it, the fireball of death that consumes the planet? Does it care? Has this bug been to the surface? Did it choose to come down here, to be with the only humans left? Or is the bug terrified of the world that it lives in, terrified to become extinct, just like the other living being inside the confines of this room?

The bug falls down from the ceiling and lands on the picture on Melissa's desk. She prepares to squash it, just as she did to a bug when she was a child living in the flurry of life in the mountains in upstate New York, but she simply stares at the bug as it walks across her picture. It stops and touches its tentacles on her son.

Melissa stands up, letting the bug find its way, letting the bug live. She moves to the window and stares at her staff. A half-dozen men and women in lab coats are looking under microscopes and making notes. Melissa grabs the notepad on her desk, the bug now gone from the picture. Her phone is flashing underneath. She sees one new text message that reads, "Going to Alex's school function. I love you."

She sets the phone down and heads to the room of scientists. She walks over to the whiteboard and writes, "1 pigeon = 1 ton of steel; 1 hole = 1 shield; We have available 19 pigeons with 36 holes; How many holes can have 4 pigeons?"

"What is that, Mrs. Mercer?" a young female scientist with glasses asks.

"Apply the pigeonhole principle."

The young scientist adjusts her glasses. Another man with a gray beard says, "Four holes with three pigeons left over."

"Exactly," Melissa says, stepping back from the whiteboard. "This means that four shields can get reinforced, which means that two quadrants will be lost, and these four shields, one per the four quadrants, can buy us maybe a month extra." She moves in closer. "The other extreme is we put all nineteen pigeons into one hole. This buys one-sixth of one quadrant eight months. So now we are faced with deciding whether we should save more people for less time or less people for more time."

"Forgive me if I am being naive, Mrs. Mercer," the young scientist says. "But why can't we get more pigeons."

"Pigeons are easy, but they represent *steel*. Where the hell are we going to get more steel?"

"Mrs. Mercer," Philip says. "The president's office has confirmed our nine a.m. meeting tomorrow."

"And how are we going to get it fast?" Melissa sets down the whiteboard marker, and then exits the room.

"Philip?" Melissa says in the hallway.

"Yes, Mrs. Mercer."

"I want to apologize for being short with you before."

"I understand, ma'am. We're all under a lot of stress."

"We're all underground, that's what we're under."

"Ma'am. I don't know anything about pigeonhole principles and all this scientific stuff, but I know that we will find a way. We're all in this together."

"You're a good man, Philip," Melissa says, putting her hands on his shoulders.

"Thank you, Mrs. Mercer. I really listened to what the president said this morning, about his talk concerning family. I think you should go be with your family. The president wanted you to fact find, to explain all this to him and his departments. Don't put the whole weight of this just on your shoulders."

"You're right. Let's meet up at six a.m. We'll get our presentation together." Melissa starts to walk away. "Oh, and Philip. You go home now too. Tell all the staff to go home."

"Thank you, Mrs. Mercer," he says. "Oh, there's a bug!" Philip goes to step on it.

"No!" she shouts, but his foot squashes it.

Miles away, two blonde girls are showing a handcrafted solar system to the captivated audience. The shorter one says, "This is the sun. Its distance from Earth is ninety-three million miles. Before

Underground Day, the sun provided light to allow photosynthesis in plants, which allowed them to grow and be the food source for animals, including humans."

The side door to the classroom opens. James walks in, still in his work suit. His hair is combed, but hints of grease are still smudged on his face.

Everyone in the audience glances at him; some parents squint their eyes, while some kids in the front row smirk.

Sitting with the kids in the front row, Brian sees his dad enter. He waves and smiles.

"Why is your dad so dirty?" Alex whispers to him.

"He was working."

James sees Janice in the middle of the crowd. They share a smile. He goes to squeeze between parents, but the woman on the end flares her nostrils as she eyes his dirty work clothes.

James retreats and stands behind the back row.

"We made our solar system using recycled paper and non-toxic glue," the taller girl says, showing the model to the crowd.

The teacher steps up on stage and starts clapping, which prompts the parents to clap and cheer.

"Thank you, Ashley and Amy, for that wonderful presentation on our solar system." The crowd simmers down. "Kids, come up here."

The dozen students go up on stage. Alex and Brian stand in the middle and smile.

"We now invite you to the open house where our students will answer questions at their different projects. I want to thank each and every one of you for coming and for supporting your children. Without your generosity and support, the generation of tomorrow would not have this opportunity to learn. Thank you."

The crowd claps even louder. The kids all bow, and the audience stands and greets them.

Brian runs to his dad and hugs him. "You made it!"

"I couldn't miss my son's big day."

Janice arrives. "That was a great show, honey. You guys did wonderful." She looks at her husband and shakes her head. "It's nice that you came, but you could've got cleaned up. These parents are all white-collar here. You know that."

He ignores her and looks at his son. "Let's see your project, tiger."

A few feet away, Alex embraces his dad. "What do you think?"

"Great work. You gave a great presentation. Just like your mom."

"I wish she came," Alex says.

"I know, buddy. We'll tell her all about it later."

Alex and his father walk to the model of the bridge.

"I like how you added the little bird on the top," Richard says.

"That was Brian's idea."

Brian and his parents come over.

"Our sons make a great team," Janice says.

Everyone laughs.

"I know they were working on this for a few weeks. I'm Richard."

"I'm Janice." They shake hands. "And this is my husband, James."

Both men shake hands. "Nice to meet you," Richard says.

"Likewise."

"Hey, UVASHIELD," Richard reads on James' uniform.

"Twelve years now."

"My wife works there," Richard says.

"Oh, which department?"

"She's the CEO."

James smiles. "Melissa Mercer?"

"That's me," a voice says.

Melissa walks in from behind.

"Mom, you made it!" Alex shouts, hugging her.

She kneels down, looks into her son's eyes, and sees herself. "Of course I made it. I'm sorry I wasn't here sooner."

She stands up. "Hi, everyone. I'm Melissa."

"These are Brian's parents, James and Janice," Richard says.

They each shake hands. Melissa studies James' smile, the dimples in his cheeks, the grease smeared across his forehead. "I know you," she says.

He points at the label on his shirt. "I work for you, ma'am."

"Please, please, call me Melissa. We're all family here."

"So *you're* the one making my husband late for dinner," Janice says.

Everyone laughs.

"She's never home for dinner either. Me and you should compare recipes," Richard adds, sending even more laughter.

"No. I saw you this morning," Melissa says. "You were fixing one of the turbines in quadrant four."

"That's me. I just got that bank back up. It's running on blood, sweat, and tears."

"Mom, look at this," Alex says, presenting the model of the bridge.

"Wow, very nice. What bridge is that?"

"The Benjamin Franklin Bridge."

"I didn't know you were working on this. Look at the little cars you made. And the water looks so blue."

"Brian did that part. I worked on the bridge."

"You did a nice job, Brian," Melissa says, looking at the nine-year-old.

"That's my boy," James says.

"Since you two missed the talk, why don't you boys give them the CliffsNotes version?" Janice says.

"What're CliffsNotes?" Alex asks.

"You have to be our age to know that," Richard says. "They were for people who didn't want to read the book in class."

"We're all getting too old," Janice adds. They all chuckle.

"The Benjamin Franklin Bridge was built one hundred nineteen years ago in nineteen twenty-six," Alex says.

"It was originally named the Delaware River Bridge," Brian continues. "It is a suspension bridge across the Delaware River connecting Philadelphia, Pennsylvania and Camden, New Jersey."

"I tried my best to match the color of the bridge's steel before Underground Day," Alex says, showing the greenish-blue structure.

"It looks great," James says. "That steel is some of the strongest ever used to make a bridge."

Melissa holds her breath.

"I love the suspension cables and the road markers," Janice says.

Melissa exhales. "What did you say?"

"Me?" James says. "Oh, the steel. That stuff is probably still standing strong out there. I wish we had some. It'd make my job easier."

Everyone chuckles except for Melissa.

"How far is the bridge from here?" she asks.

"The bridge is on the east side of Philadelphia," Brian says.

"We're under what used to be Chester, Pennsylvania. That might as well be in Europe," James says, chuckling.

"No, seriously. How many miles away is it?"

"Shoot. I would say about twenty miles. Like I said, it might as well be two thousand miles away in London."

"Oh, you must be the parents," the chubby teacher says with a smile.

They all smile and say *yes* together.

"Alex and Brian are our two best students. They love math and science."

The boys blush.

Melissa steps away and pulls out her smart tablet. Richard squints his eyes.

The two blonde girls showing their model of the solar system snicker. "Look at Brian's dad. He looks like one of those people in quadrant four," one of them says.

Melissa overhears them and looks up from her smart tablet.

A tall woman with blonde hair and wearing a business suit looks at the girls. "Why would they allow his kid to go to this school? You girls stay away from that boy."

Melissa steps over, an exaggerated smile on her face. "Oh, hi. I think we're neighbors," she says to the mother.

"Oh, really? I'm not sure I've seen you," the mother replies with an inflated smile.

"Sure. You're in quadrant…"

"…one. Number five, eight, zero. My husband and I love the place. It's so clean and the air quality is so nice."

"Oh, I'm sorry. I must have had you mistaken." Melissa goes to turn around.

"I didn't get your name," the mother says.

"It's okay. We wouldn't be friends anyway because I'm friends with that man over there who looks like he's from quadrant four."

Melissa steps away and pulls out her smart tablet. She clicks through her contacts and selects, "Control Team." She clicks, "New Message." Then she types, "Please raise temperature fifteen degrees in five, eight, zero of quadrant one."

8

The sun shines in the vivid blue sky. Birds soar. The wind tickles the lush trees. Kids play soccer on the green grass as parents watch.

There's a boy at the goal, wearing a red jersey. His hair is tousled, eyes wide. His mind focuses on the blue team kicking the ball. He takes a deep breath, the scent of dandelions lacing the air.

The blue team kicks the ball toward the goal.

Little James watches a big boy in blue handling the ball, eyeing up the goal. The only worry in the world for little James is protecting the goal.

The big kid in blue passes it to another kid, who shoots.

Little James' teammate blocks the shot, which sends his parents cheering in the crowd.

As little James looks up, the big boy in blue regains control of the ball. James notices the birds escaping from a tree.

The big boy shoots again.

"Go, James! Block the ball!" a woman yells in the crowd.

"You got it, son!" the man next to her yells.

James dives through the air, but the ball escapes his hands and enters the goal.

The ground starts shaking, tossing his body like a rag doll. Cheers change to screams. The Earth becomes angry as little James loses his footing.

A hole opens up in the middle of the field. Little James closes his eyes.

A beep blasts.

Suddenly, the red light from an alarm clock pierces James' eyes. He awakens in his bed.

Janice sits up, reaching to turn off the alarm.

"You didn't hear that?" she says, silencing it.

"Sorry." He sits up and rubs his eyes.

"What's wrong?"

"Yesterday did me in."

She rubs his back. "What's going on with this place?"

"The voltage regulators are taking too much stress from the heat."

"No, I mean this life," she says. "What are we doing down here? It's been how long?"

"Twenty years next month," he responds.

"Why are we here?"

"To keep the human race alive," he says.

"What kind of life is this? Eating simulated food. Lying in a box with a fake sun. Telling our kids how great the world once was, and now leaving them with nothing."

He puts his arm around her. "Don't worry. Life goes on. I'm just happy that I have you and Brian."

She licks her dry lips. "Do you think you would have fallen for me if we were on the surface? If we didn't have to go underground?"

"Of course."

"Really? There's not that many women left down here. I mean, you probably just asked me out because I was the only girl your age in your class."

"I asked you out because you were the only girl who laughed at my joke."

"Come on."

"It's true. I told that joke to girls on the outside, but no one laughed."

"What was it again?" she says.

"How do you make an egg roll?"

She shakes her head. "I laughed because it was so bad."

"You make an egg roll by pushing it," James says.

Janice giggles. She nudges closer to him and whispers softly, "I wish we had a real wedding with our families. I wish we could have danced in front of everyone." She exhales all the air inside her lungs. "Tell me something nice."

"When I was in elementary school," he says. "I used to love to play soccer."

"I never knew you played soccer."

"Well, I wasn't very good. But I played on our school's team. I was the goalie. My parents would go to all my games." Tears well in his eyes. "I loved soccer so much—the little things, running in the field, the birds in the trees, my parents always cheering me on, even if I lost the ball—the things that we can never have again. But then after the mess, after going underground, I had no desire to play soccer, to do anything other than work. I thought my drive was lost, but you know, last night when I saw Brian's model bridge, his enthusiasm, I knew that it wasn't lost. He inherited my desires."

She paints his palm with her fingertips. "He's such a smart kid."

A tear escapes from James' eye. "This whole life, the simulated food, the fake sun, all of it, doesn't matter. The point is, if I met you on the surface, or met you underground, it wouldn't matter. The people matter, my *family* matters."

She leans in and kisses him, tasting the salty tear on his lips.

"Mom," Brian says, opening the door.

James wipes his face and clears his throat. Janice moves over, a smile on her face.

"Yes, baby," Janice says as Brian sits next to her on the bed.

"The UV light is broken."

"Your dad will fix it, just like he fixes everything down here."

James smiles and rubs his son's head. "I'll fix anything that's broken." He stands up and puts on a T-shirt.

"Dad, can I ask you something?" Brian says.

"Sure, tiger. What's up?"

"Some of the kids in my class, they make fun of me because you get dirty at work. Their parents all dress up to go to work."

"Which kids?" Janice says. "I'll go talk to their parents."

James sits down on the edge of the bed and looks at his son. "Don't worry, tiger. Everyone has different jobs. We sometimes need people to get dirty in order to fix things that help us live down here. The other kids probably don't know too many adults who have jobs like mine."

"Some kids think we're poor."

"Hey, don't worry about credits. Your mom and dad love you so much. I work hard for you guys. I work hard to put you through that school."

Janice sits up. "You stay friends with that Alex. He's a good kid and your dad works for his mother."

"Alex seems like a good friend," James says.

"Yeah, I really like hanging out with him. He's got all the new games on his tablet."

"Oh! I almost forgot!" James jumps up and reaches into a duffel bag.

Janice and Brian smirk at each other.

"Is it a RoboDog?" Brian asks.

"Better." James removes a glass bottle filled with four ounces of clear liquid.

"What is that?" Janice asks, sliding out from under the covers.

"This right here is something special. One of the execs left it." He unscrews the cap.

"So you're stealing now," Janice says.

James swirls the liquid. "Clean. Clear. Pure water from the bedrock in quadrant one."

"What does it taste like?" Brian asks.

"It tastes like…water. Real water. None of this *purified* sewage." James hands his son the bottle. "Go on."

Brian hesitates, and then takes a sip, smacking his lips. "Tastes like…nothing."

"That's what pure water tastes like."

Brian swallows a gulp. "Here, Dad. You have some."

"No, it's for you."

"How about you, Mom?"

"You drink it, honey."

"I'll save you some." Brian swallows another big gulp, and then exhales. He gives the bottle to his mom.

Janice lets the last swallow moisten her lips as it enters her mouth. She holds it there, letting the purity unearth lost memories of her grandfather, serving her a glass of mountain spring water.

"Thanks, Dad," Brian says.

"Go to the UV light. I'll be right out to fix it."

Brian scurries away.

Janice gives her husband the bottle back as the dry, stagnant air attacks her lips.

"What's wrong?" James asks.

She exhales.

He puts his hand on her shoulder. "What is it?"

"Shifts at the ward have dried up. There are no credits for temps. And being a mom is taking everything out of me. I was thinking. Do we really have enough credits to keep sending him to that school?"

"Well, the overtime from last night will help."

"So the answer is *no*."

"Well, for this semester, we're okay."

"Maybe Alex's mom can help you. You should talk to her."

"What do you want me to do? Go in there and demand more credits?"

"Just talk to her. She's the one on top of the company. It's *her* company."

"She knows who I am."

His phone rings and his instincts make him answer it. "This is James."

"We need you in early," a male voice says. "Another one in quadrant four went down thirty minutes ago."

James looks at the clock: "7:21."

"I'll be there in twenty minutes." He ends the call.

"See, I can get more hours today," James says.

Janice crosses her arms. "This type of work is not cutting it. Another missed breakfast with your family. Maybe James' classmates are right."

"What's that supposed to mean?"

"You know what I mean." She slides under the covers.

James stands up. "I have to fix the UV lamp before going in."

Janice watches him leave.

Twenty minutes later through the guts of quadrant four, a train speeds down the track. Inside, a chunky woman wearing sweats devours a wafer. A bony man coughs, infecting the air. Two guys wearing reflective suits play a game of pong on a tablet. James stands among them, holding his pack, staring at the poster on the wall of a woman holding out a glass of orange liquid. Written above her is "Tastes like the orange juice your grandmother used to squeeze."

The man coughing keels over and vomits. The chunky woman gasps. The two men stare at their game.

James steps aside and tosses the guy a clean rag from his pack.

The train slows to a stop. The chunky woman exits as a dozen people push their way on. The people avoid the guy and the vomit. The crowd pushes James around.

An Asian woman with bleached-blonde hair stands next to him. Her perfume outweighs the stench of the vomit.

She eyes his badge for UVASHIELD. "Hey, you wanna buy some zeds?"

James shakes his head and turns to look back at the simulated orange juice.

"Buy some pussy?"

He ignores her.

"How 'bout some dick?"

He continues to look at the sign.

"Whatcha want?" she goes.

"Some credits," he replies.

She laughs. "I like you."

The train slows again. James readies his pack. The doors open as he pushes his way out.

Outside, the smell of stale air hits him. Thousands of people roam. The simulated lady in the red dress offers a card to James, so he takes it.

He trudges through the crowd. Above him, four turbines spin. A helicopter thunders by. A crowd of people swarms a vendor selling rice. James snakes through the people. A woman thrusts a plate of sushi in his face.

Two men in torn shirts start punching each other. One falls into the woman with the plate; sushi falls everywhere. People start shouting; others start clapping.

James continues walking as he passes a store labeled, "Antiques." In the window are CDs, VHS tapes, and a doll dressed like a samurai. Locked in a glass case is a smart phone, the sign reading "iPhone 4 from 2010! Working! 10,000 credits." James eyes a deflated soccer ball that says, "Used by Team USA in 2008 Olympics." Half the ball is scorched black, but there is still one section showing the original white color.

"Who wants that shit?" Chop says.

James beholds the fresh curls in Chop's mustache. "Look at those curls today."

"Why do they keep calling me when I'm sleeping?"

"I could use the credits," James says.

Both start walking through the crowd.

"I could use the sleep," Chop says. "Money, or should I say *credits*, is only good now for shit that we don't need."

"I need it for my son's school."

"Let him go to public school," Chop says. "Hell, we went to public school."

"We didn't have to worry about getting every letter of Hepatitis," James says.

"Ahh, things have changed, brother."

They move past an arcade. A guy with no arms and no legs shows a sign that reads, "Find out the truth. The government is lying to us."

A gray-haired guy jumps in front of James and Chop. "The government is lying to us. They know we are all sitting ducks down here. Demand answers!"

"Get a job, you filthy bum," Chop says, muscling past him.

"Look up there! See!" the gray-haired guy shouts, gesturing to a large display above their heads showing the news.

The female newscaster—brunette, bold, buxom—addresses the camera, her voice barely recognizable past the noise of the gathering. "Leaks from an individual inside the government suggest that there are secret, closed-door meetings going on about an expiration date in the very near future. We are treating these as just rumors at the moment."

James and Chop walk toward a set of boarded-up buildings. Painted on the wood is graffiti depicting the sun with devil horns and glaring eyes.

"This whole quadrant gives me the creeps," James says. "Why do the turbines keep dying here?"

Chop shakes his head. "Everything is dying in here."

Both men see three out of four turbines rotating fifty yards away. The fourth is stopped with a red light flashing. Reeko and Bones are checking their tools at the base of the service ladder.

"Hey, how'd the round of drinks go last night?" James asks.

"That cheapskate couldn't pay the bill afterwards. I ended up using my hard-earned credits."

"Figures," James says. "Hey, what was that Vegas story you were trying to tell me?"

"Vegas story? The one about the blind stripper?"

James laughs. "What the hell was that place called *Vegas*?"

"A place where your secrets were safe."

"Hey, girls. I was ready to call the dogs after you," Reeko says, handing them hardhats.

"Why can't we fix the turbines over in one or six?" James says, looking up at the rusty blades.

"This shit is slave labor," Chop says. "Just cause I was born closest to Asia doesn't mean I work for a sweat shop. I have time off coming."

"It don't matter if you girls were in the middle of jerking off. It'd take an act of Congress to excuse you."

The sound of a chopper invades. The guys duck. Papers from Bones' open pack blow around.

"Who ordered the pizza?" Chop says.

The chopper is the same white model with UVASHIELD plastered on its side. It lowers down, hovering five feet above the ground.

Inside, Melissa connects eyes with James and shows him a glimpse of the secrets swirling in her soul. His heart starts racing.

Once the chopper touches down, the door opens and Philip runs out, his hair blowing. "Who's in charge here?"

They all raise their hands.

"The boss needs James Wilson for a special project," Philip continues.

"We got a turbine out up there, and James is our best guy," Reeko says.

"The boss doesn't care."

James looks at Reeko and grins. He returns the hard hat to him.

"I gotta go too," Chop says. "The boss needs me to show her a good time."

"You can show that turbine a good time," Reeko says.

"I'll fix this shit," Bones says. "No problem."

Chop gives James the thumbs up.

"Hurry," Philip says.

James follows Philip to the helicopter.

Inside, Melissa shakes his hand. "How are you this morning?"

"Tired. What's this all about?" James says, eyeing up Lance in the rear of the chopper.

Lance cocks his gun.

"Let's go! We got him!" Melissa shouts into the headset and twirls her finger to the pilot.

James holds his breath. Philip hands him a headset and helps him buckle up. The chopper takes off.

"Have you ever been read into a security clearance, James?" Melissa asks.

"Security clearance? Don't we have to sign something at work?"

"This is above that, a *government* security clearance."

The chopper flies high above the crowd. James sees the display showing the same female newscaster. On screen is "Government Conspiracy?"

Stones and refuse hit the chopper. Lance nudges Melissa. "Ma'am, the glass."

James eyes his bulging biceps. "Why are they hitting us?" James asks.

"We're hated, James," Lance says. "Especially in this quadrant. You should know that."

"Mrs. Mercer—" James starts to say.

"Please, call me Melissa. Our sons are best friends. We're family here."

Philip squints his eyes as he prepares paperwork.

"What is going on?" James says. "Is everything okay with my family?"

"Your family is fine, James. But they may not be fine for long; *we all* may not be fine for long."

"I don't understand."

Philip hands him a stack of papers. "Initial here, here, and here. And sign here," he says, pointing with a pen at boxes.

James sees, "Office of the President of the United States of America" in bold font with thousands of lines of small print.

"What am I signing?" he asks.

"Just sign it," Melissa says. "We don't have much time."

"I'm sorry, but I don't know who you think I am. I'm just a technician."

"James," Melissa says, leaning forward. "You have a very smart son. He's going to be someone special someday."

"Thank you. Your son too, ma'am. I mean, Melissa," James says, smirking.

"Just sign that thing. I'll explain everything when we get there."

"Where are we going?" James asks.

"A meeting with the president."

James clutches the pen even tighter.

9

The large sign reads, "Entering the New White House. All communication devices must be turned off." James pulls out his smart phone.

Philip nods.

Before James powers it down, he sees a picture of his family. His wife's soft smile, his son's easy eyes hold on to the electrical charge in the pixels inside the screen, but then they die.

The chopper approaches the bay door. James sees the turrets, the armed men pacing the catwalk, and the bodies inside the control room.

Inside the bay, James stares at the turbines rotating. "Who fixes these turbines? I didn't even see them on our service map."

"They never need to be fixed," Melissa says. "They only purchase new ones from us."

The chopper enters and lands in its designated spot—bay 12.

When they step out, Ross greets them. "Thanks for coming early." He eyes James' blue work suit. "Who is this?"

"He's my guest," Melissa says.

James swallows.

Lance stays back with the pilot as the others make their way inside.

As they walk into the corridor, the armed men guarding the doorway stare through James.

"We need a private conference room for a few minutes," Melissa says.

"Right this way," Ross says.

They arrive at a doorway, the blinds drawn, the seal of the president proudly on display. Ross turns on the lights as Philip goes inside.

"Philip, please wait for us outside," Melissa says.

"Uh, okay," he says, his brow creased.

James takes a deep breath, the cleanest, purest, most oxygen-rich breath he's ever taken underground. His mind melts, the thought of his family in front of him.

Melissa shuts the door. Both sit down.

"Does this have anything to do with what they're saying on the news?" James asks, looking at the arrows clutched by the eagle on the wall.

"What are they saying on the news?" Melissa says.

"The end is near."

Melissa exhales through her lips, making a sound.

James squints his eyes, his stomach sinking.

"Well, first of all, don't listen to the news." She inhales a deep breath. "A scientist was recently killed outside wearing a UVASUIT."

"It was just a faulty temperature control on the suit, right?"

"Well, that's what we assumed it was at first. But then, I had our R&D department comb through the data, looking for trends, looking for abnormalities. Based on our previous models, the current shields which protect the air flow for the entire underground should have been able to withstand temps for—"

"Ten years, right?"

"Right. And then during these ten years, we would have time to engineer a new shield solution based on our current data. But based on new models after this incident, we were off, way off."

"How much?"

"We're looking at..." Melissa squeezes the armrest. "...six days left."

"No," James exhales, his voice echoing inside the confined room. The talons on the eagle sharpen; its face engulfs into flames. James reaches for his smart phone, his palms sweaty, his heart pounding.

A knock sounds at the door. Ross peeks his head in. "The president is ready."

"I have to call my wife," James says, clutching his phone.

"No electronic communication devices!" Ross shouts.

Melissa stands up and walks over to him. "I can't believe it either. I'm sorry. I'm so sorry."

"What am I doing here? Why did you tell me this?"

"I'll explain everything in a few minutes."

Melissa stands up and opens the door as James follows her.

They walk through the corridors. James sees the seal of the president around every corner, the face of the eagle burning, the eyes of the bird glaring. His wife's face and his son's innocence race through his mind. How long would it take him to get back to them, to protect them? Could they escape to the service location that only a select few know about, buried the furthest away from the surface? Could they survive?

Inside the conference room, President Brooks and Secretary Dunner are already sitting in their seats. The scientists are sitting with charts and graphs stacked in front of them.

Secretary Dunner squints his eyes as he stares down James.

"Mrs. Mercer. Please sit," President Brooks says.

She listens to him as James and Philip sit behind her.

"Only speak when spoken to," Philip whispers to James.

The president leans forward in his chair. "Well, you're right, Mrs. Mercer. I hate to say it. I wish this was some twisted joke, but our scientists have confirmed your results." He glances at the scientists at the conference table, who nod. "I don't know about you, but I can't shake this. I said a prayer to God last night when I was lying awake in the dark, lying next to my wife, lying in the room next to my children. I asked God for a chance to survive. We *must* survive."

Secretary Dunner shakes his head, a smirk on his face.

"Please tell me that God answered my prayers," the president continues.

Melissa hands a flash drive to Ross. He loads it into the computer.

James sees Secretary Dunner staring at him. His eyes pierce him, go through him, grip his soul. James scrunches his toes inside his work shoes as Secretary Dunner's eyes puncture his veins like a nurse stealing blood. James looks away, but the eyes of evil still haunt him.

Melissa stands up and grabs the pointer from Ross.

"Since our meeting yesterday, I worked every scenario, looked at all our resources, consulted with our top scientists. Before Underground Day, when just a girl in elementary school, my father was a professor of Mathematics at the University of Pennsylvania. One day at home when I was playing with a ball, it rolled into his study and under his desk. I remember going inside and seeing the image of a pigeon inside the open book on his desk. I thought it was a bird-watching book; heck, I was only about seven years old. But I remember reading the binding of the book and it said, *Theory of Computation*. And on that page was a mathematical concept called the *pigeonhole principle*. Now, forty years later, after all the mess, after my parents' passing, that little pigeon will be the key to determining who and how many humans can survive."

Melissa switches to the first slide, which shows five holes and six pigeons. "The concept is simple, if there are n pigeons and m holes with n greater than m, the pigeonhole principle tells us that at least one hole must have more than one pigeon. So in our situation, let's say that one pigeon equals one ton of steel. In our stockpile, we have nineteen tons of steel, or nineteen pigeons. Let's say that one hole equals one shield."

She clicks the slide showing an animation of pigeons in a line next to the map of the underground. "Therefore, there are thirty-six total holes in our underground country. So the problem is, how do we distribute these tons of steel to sustain and to allow harvesting of more steel within this timeframe—a self-serving, renewable cycle? If we spread out the nineteen tons of steel, we can fully reinforce four shields in four quadrants with a shield seventy-five percent protected in a fifth quadrant. Based on the rate of the temperature increase and shield workload, these four quadrants with one shield reinforced would perish in thirty days, and this fifth quadrant would last about fourteen days. This does not allow us enough time to harvest more steel to get a cycle going of sustainable protection for the shields. The other extreme, we could put all nineteen tons of steel into one hole, this would provide part of this one quadrant eight months, but there is no way to harvest enough steel from the sources we currently use within reach of our existing UVASUITs.

"So you're saying we're doomed?" the president says.

"This is ridiculous," Secretary Dunner says. "Pigeons into holes. I think we need to bring our own scientists to the front here."

Melissa clutches the pointer. "I'm saying that if we had a source of hardened steel, we could reinforce, and more importantly, could sustain the requirements of three shields in quadrant two. These shields are our best bet with location and current workload."

"What does this get us?" the president asks.

"I calculated the oxygen consumption, underground air temperature, CO_2 exhalation. We're looking at eight hundred individuals, maybe a thousand."

"So you're saying that ninety-eight thousand Americans are going to expire? How are we supposed to select these people?"

"I wish I knew, sir."

"Let's start with eliminating the riffraff in quadrant four," Secretary Dunner says.

"Robert!" the president shouts.

Melissa exhales. "Sir, these thousand individuals can still only survive with *steel*. And we don't have the supply of steel."

"Where do we get more steel?" the president says.

Melissa clicks to the next slide. It shows an image of the Benjamin Franklin Bridge. "One of my top technicians can comment on this." She looks at James.

"Yes, sir," James says, his voice cracking. He clears his throat. "I started with UVASHIELD reinforcing the shields with steel, and now I am one of the lead technicians for turbine repair. The steel on the shields needs to be extremely dense, the strongest and most durable metal available. The Ben Franklin Bridge is still standing; that steel is *strong*. We can harvest it and create a cycle to sustain the shields."

"That structure might as well be on the moon," Secretary Dunner says. "We looked at that when we went underground. It's too far."

"It *was* too far," Melissa says. "But my R&D team has been designing a new prototype of our suits, a new, reinforced version."

"Ha! Reinforced suits!" Secretary Dunner shouts. "You want to put all our lives on the quality of your suits?"

Melissa clicks the next slide, which shows a countdown timer: "5 days, 23 hours, 48 minutes." The seconds are counting down from 32.

"Who will lead this effort?" the president says.

"I will go," Melissa says.

"You haven't laid the steel, ma'am," Philip says. "You've only theorized about it."

President Brooks leans forward in his seat. "Well, I expect you to select the best team of technicians available. While you are selecting your team, we have a tough situation to deliver to the American people. *I* have a tough situation. It must be a lottery system, but until we have every detail worked out, every answer prepared, none of this gets out. If the media gets a hold of this, we're going to have a civil war on our hands." The president looks at Secretary Dunner. "I remind everyone of their security obligations." The president looks at James. "I take it your man is cleared."

"Yes, sir," Melissa says. "He was read in on the way here."

"Well…uh, I didn't get your name," the president says.

"Wilson, sir. James Wilson."

"Well, Mr. Wilson. I task you with assembling a team of the best. The human race is riding on this team." The president exhales.

"Aristotle said that the whole is greater than the sum of its parts. But is the President of the United States greater than the sum of his team, the sum of each of you in this room? I'm just a figure here. I'm really just a product of each and every one of you in this room. I ask that each of you do this not for me, but for you and your families. Now go. Let's meet again in eight hours with an action plan I can deliver to the American people. The clock is ticking."

Everyone stares at the digits on the screen: "5 days, 23 hours, 45 minutes, 10 seconds"… "9 seconds"…

10

Orange lights fly by the window of the chopper as it thunders forward.

James sits inside, watching the lights, his eyes frozen, his mind null. Across from him, Melissa messages her chief scientist on her smart tablet. Philip sits next to the pilot and organizes his notes from the meeting. Squeezing a stress ball, Lance stares through the rear window of the chopper.

Turbulence rocks them, but James doesn't blink. He removes his smart phone. "Can I use this now?"

Melissa nods.

He turns the device on. The picture of his wife and son is still there. They stare at him from inside the pixels, watching his stone face, his dry lips. They are just as he remembers them from an hour ago, except for one grave difference—their faces are on fire, their flesh burning. He closes his eyes and stares at the darkness in front of him.

James feels pressure on his knee. He opens his eyes. Melissa is offering her hand.

Outside the window, dozens of people enjoy a lush park. A woman and child walk a Chihuahua-size RoboDog. Guys play a game of polo. Kids kick a soccer ball. Simulated lanterns shine lights throughout the area.

"We're leaving quadrant three and going to be flying through four," the pilot says.

Lance sits up. "I remind everyone to stay away from the glass."

The chopper slows down and flies through a large bay door. Down below, a dozen armed military members screen people walking through the quadrant passage.

Past the bay door, light becomes dark. The stench of sewage invades. Water drips. Lights flicker. Hundreds of people fifty feet below holler and push to exit quadrant four.

Someone throws a shoe at the chopper window.

"I'm sorry that I pulled you in like that," Melissa says.

James exhales.

"I thought you wanted to call your family."

"Why did you do this to me?" James says.

Melissa narrows her eyes and moves her hair aside. "I'm sorry, James."

"Why did you want me to come with you today?"

"From our meeting last night, with our kids' presentation about the bridge."

James shakes his head. "Why would you do this to me? I didn't ask to speak today. Who do you think I am?"

Lance grips his pistol and leans forward.

Melissa pushes Lance back. "James, I'm sorry. I wish I could change all of this. I wish I didn't have to find this out."

"I'm just a technician. Just a guy trying to provide for his family. I think you got me confused with someone else."

"I'm not asking you do anything."

"Sure you are. You want me to go on a death trip. I'm not stupid. And I'm not your puppet."

Philip turns around.

"I have work to do," James says. "Just put me down here."

The pilot turns around and looks at James fiddling with the door. The chopper bobbles.

Lance grabs James' arm. "Sir, sit in your seat."

James resists and keeps yanking at the door.

The pilot looks at Melissa, who nods.

Melissa pulls Lance back and shakes her head.

The pilot brings the chopper closer to the ground as stones hit the glass.

"Sir," Philip says to James. "You must come with us. Your job assignment is no longer out here."

"I quit!" he shouts, finally getting the door open.

"Let him go," Melissa says to Philip.

The chopper hovers three feet above an open area. The wind rushes inside. Melissa holds down her papers.

"You have signed a security agreement with the United States Government," Philip says. "You *must* not speak a word of any of this."

James jumps out and rolls onto the ground. The chopper lifts up and speeds over him.

The grubby old man with the scarred face picks James up. "What'd you do, young man?"

"I saw the wizard of Oz."

James runs through the crowd and dials his wife on the phone. The signal dies. He bumps into a woman in a red dress handing out cards.

The grubby old man points at James. "He is the devil! The devil is among us!"

Another man glares at James. Two women gasp.

James runs through the mob and dials the number again. The phone connects.

"Hello?" Janice says.

"Honey, pack the bags. I'm going to get Brian."

"What? What's going on?"

"Something big is going down. Remember that place I told you about, deep down with the food and supplies. We have to get there."

"Does this have anything to do with the news?"

"What's the news saying?" he asks.

There's a skinny guy on a scooter up ahead. James pushes the guy off. He jumps on and zips through the crowd, nearly hitting a RoboDog. He juggles his phone in his hand, trying to steer.

"Something about the end being near," Janice says.

James swerves around a vendor cart. The phone falls and smashes on the concrete.

"Shit!" He leaves it behind and continues racing through the crowd.

Miles away through the corridors, the helicopter lowers to land into a bay. Melissa stares through the window at the illuminated UVASHIELD logo and at the tagline, "Protecting the New America."

When the chopper touches down, the pilot kills the engine. He steps out and opens the side and rear doors.

Lance hops out and helps Melissa. "Ma'am, do you want me to pick him up?"

"What have I done?" she mouths, still staring at the logo.

Philip steps out. "Security can pick him up, ma'am," he says, looking from Melissa to Lance.

"Did I really think that it would be this easy?" she continues, staring at the dirty concrete.

"Ma'am, you are so strong for all of us," Philip says. "Don't let this guy get away and ruin everything."

"How's he going to ruin everything? Just let him go. Let him be with his family."

Lance bites down hard on the tip of his thumb.

Melissa walks inside with Philip as Lance goes toward a side entrance.

"What do you want me to do?" Philip asks.

"Go check on the new suits. They have to be ready."

"Who's going to lead the effort?" Philip asks.

Melissa stops walking, the UVASHIELD logo just above her head. She stares at the word *Protecting*.

11

A soccer ball soars through the air, floating for what seems to be hours. The goalie jumps, arms raised, but the ball sneaks through his hands and enters the goal.

"Soccer was the most popular sport in the world," the chubby teacher says.

The students watch the video on the projector screen. Alex and Brian are the most interested—their eyes wide and their pencils ready.

"Is that what they played at the Super Bowl?" Alex asks.

"No, they played football at the Super Bowl. While football was the most popular sport in America, the world loved soccer. Everywhere from South America to Mexico to Europe loved to compete for the ultimate prize, the World Cup."

"Where are all the people in South America and Mexico and Europe?" Brian asks.

"Well, Brian. You know about the world," the teacher says, a frown on her face.

A knock sounds at the door. A young secretary comes in. The class watches her move toward the teacher.

James steps inside, his eyes fixed on his son. Brian smiles.

"Ma'am, Brian Wilson's father is here," the secretary whispers. "He needs to take Brian home. There's a family emergency."

"Of course," she replies. "Brian, your father is here to pick you up."

The two blonde girls snicker when they see James. Brian packs his books.

The teacher moves to the girls. "Stop it, you two," she mouths to them. "Excuse me, Mr. Wilson. While Brian is collecting his things, would you have a minute to tell the class about your job? We have been learning about different careers in the new America."

"Uh, okay." James steps toward the front of the class and stands in the light of the projector. "I am a technician for UVASHIELD. I maintain, troubleshoot, and repair issues with the turbine ventilation systems."

"You hear that class. That sounds like a very important job," the teacher says. "Why did you get into this field?"

The video on the projector starts playing. The image of the soccer ball projects onto James. He stares at the light as it enters his eyes and sneaks into his mind. The light retrieves memories buried so deeply that James stops breathing. He sees the soccer ball flying toward him, feels the earthquake, smells the fire. The ground opens in the middle of the field and steals his teammates.

"Mr. Wilson, why did you get into this field?"

"I was playing soccer. I tried to block the ball. My parents were watching me."

The teacher squints her eyes. The two blonde girls laugh, which prompts more laughter from the class.

James steps out of the light. Brian meets him with his backpack at the door. They leave the class as the kids laugh louder.

"Dad, what's wrong?"

"I'm sorry, tiger. I'm just stressed."

"Where are we going? Is mom okay?"

"Mom is fine. We're just going on a little trip."

They exit the corridor past the secretary and go to the scooter.

"Cool scooter. Will we fit?"

"Let's go, son."

James helps Brian on the back.

"Hold on," James says as he gears up the scooter.

Through the arteries of the underground and inside the offices of UVASHIELD, Melissa is wearing protective eyeglasses and is standing behind four inches of glass. She's fixated on a silver-colored UVASUIT hanging on a rack. A test dummy rests inside with a smile drawn onto its plastic face.

Two scientists hold fire extinguishers, while another one holds a smart tablet. The one with the tablet hits a button; an inferno of fire attacks the suit.

Melissa squints her eyes, the light reflecting off them.

When the fire stops, the suit is charred black. The smile on the dummy has melted into a frown. The scientist checks data on the smart tablet.

"Give me good news?" Melissa says.

"It's still failing to handle the temps."

Melissa throws her glasses on the ground, shattering them.

Philip walks over. "Mrs. Mercer, sorry, but you have a visitor."

"Who is it?" she says, fire in her eyes. When she looks beyond Philip, she sees the trimmed beard, oval glasses, and furrowed brow of her husband.

"Where have you been all day?" he says. "I can't get a hold of you."

Melissa steps toward him. "Please take five, everyone."

"What is going on here?" Richard says. "Why did you throw those glasses?"

The people leave the area.

Melissa moves closer to her husband and puts her hands around him. "I'm sorry, honey."

He flicks her away. "What are you sorry about?"

"There's something going on."

"What? The news is saying something about the end being near."

Melissa shakes her head.

"Tell me what's going on," he says.

"I'm under a security clearance."

"Come on, Melissa. Do you think I'm some bum in quadrant four? Or some snitch who's going to leak something to the media? I'm your husband. I'm the father of your child. Alex is still in class. He's not here with us. So, tell me, for your family, what the hell is going on?"

Melissa moves in close. She sees her reflection in her husband's glasses. His masculine scent lulls her. She closes her eyes and falls into his arms. She's no longer a CEO, an engineer, a boss. She's a wife, a mother. The weight of the Earth above her head comes down upon her body. Her vision clouds and her muscles surrender.

"The world is on my shoulders," she says before passing out.

12

A suitcase is open on the bed. The sound of a drip fills the cramped room.

Drip... Drip... Drip...

Janice sits on a chair, listening to the steady drip. The phone lies next to her, its menu showing six dialed calls to her husband—all unanswered. Janice now waits, the longest wait of her life.

The front door opens.

She springs from her chair.

James hustles inside as Brian follows.

"Oh God," Janice says.

"Get only the essentials. And pack as many wafers as we can fit."

"James, what's going on?"

"Quick. Just grab everything you can." James runs into the back bedroom.

Janice looks at her son and combs his frazzled hair with her fingers. "Are you okay, baby?"

"I'm okay, Mom. But Dad is saying some weird stuff."

"Weird stuff? Like what?"

"I don't know. About going somewhere deep underground. And he started talking about soccer in front of the class when he came to get me. The kids were laughing at him."

"You stay here, baby. I'm going to go talk to Dad."

Janice moves into the bedroom. Inside, James is rifling through a drawer. He stops when he finds a lockbox.

"What are you doing?" she asks.

He ignores her, opens the box, and then removes a pistol.

"James!" Janice shouts.

He drops the gun and stops moving. He looks into his wife's eyes.

"What is wrong with you?" she says.

"What?"

"All this. What the hell is going on?"

He puts the gun back into the box and locks it. "I'm sorry," he says, shaking his head.

"What happened today at work?"

"I met with the president at the New White House."

"James, if you're going to sit there and lie to me, you might as well—"

"The heat is going to kill us. The news reports are correct. Five days left, and then we're all dead."

Janice's heart stops. She holds her breath. "What?"

"Melissa Mercer pulled me off my job this morning. She had me go with her to the briefing."

"Why isn't the president on the smart tablets?"

James holds his wife in his arms. "He will be in a few hours. He's going to announce that we can only save a thousand people. There's going to be a lottery."

"We just saw Melissa last night. She didn't say any of this."

"You think I can just tell anybody? They made me sign some security agreement. But it all doesn't matter."

"What are you talking about? Where do you want us to go? Where are we running to?"

"That emergency bunker beneath quadrant four. The one Chop and I worked on. If we can get down there before this news breaks, we might have a chance. We can defend the doorway. Kill anything that moves."

"Stop! Just stop!" Janice breaks away from her husband's arms. "You're talking like a crazy person. What are they saying? What is the solution?"

"Brian's model of the bridge last night. That's the only way we can survive. We need to harvest steel from the bridge to reinforce some shields."

"If these shields are reinforced, how many people will they protect?"

"A thousand. That's it. That's one percent of all of us down here, one percent of the whole world." James squeezes some socks on the bed.

"What does she want you to do?" Janice asks.

"Well, she didn't come out and say it, but I know she wants me to go. That's a suicide mission."

"She said it was a suicide mission?"

"They have some new suits they're designing. Listen, Janice. We need to get out of here before the mess. This is our only chance. I'm going to save this family."

"There you go again. You're talking crazy again. How do you expect to save your family by going against everyone who is trying to save us all? If we escape to the bunker, we might as well be dead. If you help them, they will *have to* save you. And they'll have to save me and Brian. We can be part of the thousand."

James sits down on the bed and starts crying. "Ever since I was a kid, I learned the hard way that we're all in this ourselves. That day when the earthquake hit, no one was there to save me. I had to watch my mother and my father get swallowed by the Earth. And then after that, I lived in one of the refugee camps until we were forced underground. People were sick. Food was scarce. I remember crying for my parents for months." He clears his throat. "We're not in this together. We have to take matters into our own hands to survive."

Janice rests her hand on his back. "Listen to me. This is different. You're an adult, a technician, a family man. You're not a helpless kid. You have some of the most important skills to protect your family, to protect all of us down here. Don't be afraid. Fear is evil. Fear is what will get you killed. If we run out that door, if we run away from everyone, we might as well use that gun on ourselves."

Brian walks in, tears in his eyes. "Mom, I'm scared."

Janice pulls him close to her side.

James sits up, trying to hide his tears. "Hey, tiger. I'm sorry about today. I'm scared too. But I'm here now. Your mom's here. And we're going to do everything we can to protect you."

13

The sun shines in the blue sky over the city. Cars flow through the streets. People window-shop on the sidewalk. The smell of sunscreen causes Melissa to look up from her book, causes her to stop chewing the turkey and avocado sandwich in her hand. She tracks the scent to the two young women next to her with the bags from Victoria's Secret.

Melissa swallows the bite of her sandwich as she picks up the place in her book, but the coffee cup in front of her suddenly clatters. Her seat starts shaking. She holds her plate.

People scream. Horns beep. The angry Earth yells.

A taxicab swerves onto the sidewalk. It plows into a man wheeling a carriage six feet from Melissa.

She goes to help, but the Earth opens up. People scamper. The Earth swallows the young women next to her.

Melissa crawls forward and sees the baby carriage pinned under the taxi.

The cries of a baby steal her breath.

The ground shakes Melissa away, but she keeps crawling. Reaching the carriage, she sees the face of her baby, her Alex. Next to the carriage is Richard, trapped under the car.

Suddenly, the weight of the car crushes her body. The pain is so intense it's beyond pain. Melissa closes her eyes.

"Mom?" Alex says.

Suddenly, she opens her eyes.

She's in her office, on the couch. Alex is standing over her.

"Baby, what happened?"

"You passed out, Mom."

"Are you okay?" Richard says from her desk.

"How long have I been out? Where is everyone?"

"You were out for almost two hours. The doctor said you are under too much pressure."

Melissa sits up and reaches for Alex to sit next to her.

"Weird stuff's happening, Mom," Alex says, sitting down next to her.

"Like what, baby?"

"On the way here in the train, there were military guys everywhere. And there were all these people screaming about the end of the world. And even at school, Brian's dad came and said some weird stuff."

"Brian's dad?"

"Yeah, he started talking about soccer when Miss Katman asked him about his job. It was kinda funny. He took Brian away. They looked like they were in a hurry."

Melissa squeezes him tightly as she looks at Richard. "What time is it? I have to prepare for another meeting. And check on the UVASUITs."

Richard scoots his chair over to the couch. "Honey, I know what's happening."

"How do you know?"

"Philip told me."

She looks down at a crack in the floor.

He takes her hand. "You don't have to do this all yourself. You have a smart team around you. Don't take on the world by yourself."

She rubs her temples. "It's my job. This is my company. The people down here, the president, they all rely on my products and services."

"I know they do. But *we* rely on you too—your husband, your son. Don't forget about those people right in front of you."

She smiles. "I never will."

A knock sounds at the door.

"Come in," Melissa says.

Philip opens the door and sees the family. "Mrs. Mercer. How are you feeling? Do you want me to call someone?"

"No, Philip. It's okay. Thank you. How is everything going?"

"The lab is making great progress with the suits. We're all working one hundred and ten percent. I have a visitor here."

"Who?"

"Mr. Wilson. And he brought his family."

"His family?"

"Yes, ma'am. He's asking to speak with you."

Melissa looks at her husband. She feels her son's warmth against her skin. "Let them in."

Philip leaves.

"You're not in this alone," Richard says. Melissa hugs him.

Philip opens the door, letting James, Janice, and Brian inside.

"Hey, Alex!" Brian says.

"Hey!" Alex stands up and walks to him.

Philip seals the six individuals in the room.

"Ma'am," James says. "I want to apologize for the way I acted before."

Melissa stands up. "We're all handling the pressure in different ways. I understand."

"I guess I'm scared of everything, scared of the future. My first instinct was to run."

"I think that's all our first instincts," Richard says.

"But I've been speaking with my family," James says, holding Janice next to his side. "I'm not going to run; I'm going to stay here and help us."

"Thank you, James," Melissa says.

They shake hands, squeezing at the same strength.

"We do have two stipulations though," Janice says.

Melissa nods. "Okay."

"If my husband is going to help you with this, if you want him to go out there to work, you must promise me that you will bring him back to me, to us, safely."

"I'm going to do everything in my power to ensure his safety. What's the other stipulation?"

"You must *guarantee* that Brian, James, and I are included in the thousand survivors."

Melissa glances at her husband, and then looks back at Janice. "Everyone's asking me that. It's up to the president's system."

"We'll walk right out of here then," Janice says with fire in her eyes. "Come on, you know you have pull. My husband is taking all the risk."

"Okay. I'll make sure that you, Brian, and James are on the list I give to the president."

"When is the president going to be making the statement?" Janice asks.

She glances at the clock on the wall: "2:35." "Our meeting is in two hours. He's planning to make the statement right after."

"Two hours?" James says. "I need my team together."

"Who do you want? Remember, we're all counting on you."

James looks at the picture of a redwood tree on the wall. There are two branches forming curlicues.

14

Chop curls his mustache inside a dirty mirror. Grease covers his cheek. Sweat stains the collar of his uniform.

"Does that thing get you laid?" Bones says next to him, staring at the mustache.

"The ladies love this thing." A bottle in front of Chop on the bar reads, "Simulated Beer."

Across the bar, a drunken guy pounds a bottle down. The bartender grabs another and opens it for the drunk.

On the middle shelf are dozens of bottles labeled, "Whiskey Mix." On the top shelf is a bottle of Jack Daniel's Old Tennessee Whiskey locked in a cabinet.

A woman in a red dress walks in. The bartender gives her a stack of cards.

"Hey, Chop," Reeko says. "There's your lady."

"Hey, they have all the right parts," Chop says. "She'd put the *screw* into screw."

"Hey, Miss. Or I mean, *Simulated Miss*," Bones goes.

She looks at him.

"My friend here wants to know if you want a mustache ride."

Chop studies her pale white skin, lost eyes, red lips.

"Card?" she says, offering Chop one.

"Don't take it, Chop. It's a trick," Reeko says.

"Boys, this one's got the marketing chip in her, not the prostitute," the bartender says.

"Look at her eyes," Chop says. "You can tell a horny geek in a lab made her."

"This coupon offers you admission to the Ghost Bar," she says.

"I'm already in the Ghost Bar, baby," Chop says, moving toward her with his s-beer.

"Chop, get your ass back in your chair," Reeko says.

Chop reaches over and pets her hair with his thick, callused hands. "Wow. You're beautiful."

Bones laughs.

Chop caresses her face, and then strokes her neck. He goes in for a kiss. Suddenly, she opens her mouth and emits a piercing sound. Chop falters back as everyone looks.

"The rape whistle?" Bones says.

"I'm going to make them take her out of your paycheck," Reeko says.

The bartender goes around, opens the back of her head, and then fiddles with some wires. The sound finally ends.

"Goddamn woman," the drunken guy shouts. "She sounds worse than my ex-wife."

Chop retreats to his seat.

"Thank you," the woman says in a chipper voice.

"Go do your job," the bartender says.

The woman slinks out of the bar with her stack of promotional cards.

Chop swallows the last swig of his drink. "Another round?"

"Hey, only one s-beer was the offer," Reeko says.

"I gotta hit the head," Bones says, walking to the back.

The bartender looks at the two guys.

"Alright, I'll buy us another round," Chop says.

The bartender goes to fetch the drinks.

Chop looks at the empty seat next to him. "Where the hell is James?"

"He's probably whirling around quadrant one being fed grapes by that colony of Polynesian women," Reeko says.

"Aww, that would be nice," Chop says. "Hey, let's go to the brothel."

Reeko shakes his head. "I think that mustache is messing with your mojo, man."

On the television, the female newscaster cuts in. "Breaking News" flashes on the screen.

"Put this up," Reeko says.

The bartender delivers three bottles of s-beer, and then turns up the volume on the television.

"Reports of a secret meeting with the president and top members of the government and industry are rumored to be occurring as we speak. Some speculate that this further confirms that America is in trouble. No official word yet from the New White House."

"Something big is going on," Reeko says.

"Ahh, I've heard all that shit before. Even before Underground Day, they were talking about all these secret wars and government conspiracies."

"How old are you, Chop? A hundred a ten?"

Bones returns. "Chop was around when the French invaded America."

"You mean the British," Chop says. "That was seventeen seventy-six."

Reeko finishes a long gulp of his drink. "I told you. This guy's a relic."

A woman screams outside the bar.

"See, I'm not the only one who thinks that chic is pretty," Chop says.

A whirlwind thunders above the bar. The wind blows napkins and sends the smell of sewage toward the patrons. The drunken guy runs out and shouts, "The truth is up there! They know!"

Chop goes out and sees the chopper hovering fifty feet above the bar. The UVASHIELD logo proudly displays.

The drunken guy throws a beer bottle at the window.

Chop hides behind a canopy, the shattered glass showering the crowd.

James peers over the side of the open chopper door. "Chop!"

"What the hell?" Chop shouts.

"I need you guys!" James yells.

"What?"

"I need you guys! We have to go back to the plant!"

A guy throws a stone up at the chopper. Bones tackles him.

James moves to avoid the hit as the chopper dips. He falls out, dangling over the edge. The crowd gasps. Finally, he pulls himself up.

Reeko comes out. "What's going on?"

"James needs us," Chop goes.

"He's going to get mauled up there," Reeko says.

Chop looks over at the woman in the red dress. He runs over to her and opens up the panel in the back of her head.

"Enough with her!" Reeko shouts.

Chop adjusts some switches. She bobs her head up and down.

"I know it's in here. This model should still have it," Chop says, pressing some more buttons.

Her mouth forms a smirk. "Hey, baby." Then the piercing sound emits from her mouth, overpowering the sound of the helicopter. People start eyeing the woman. Chop pulls a cable and plugs it into a different port.

The woman in red starts whipping the cards at the crowd like a ninja whipping stars. She hits the drunken guy in the head, which sends him running away.

Chop points toward an open area. "Over there! Come down!"

The chopper lowers down thirty yards away, while the woman distracts the crowd. James jumps out.

"What's going on, brother?" Chop asks.

"Something big is happening."

A guy grabs a broken broom and charges at the chopper.

Bones runs over and jumps him. The broom handle hits the blades, which blasts woodchips everywhere.

They all duck.

"Let's go, guys," James says.

Reeko muscles in. Bones follows. Then Chop makes it inside. When James steps in, the drunken guy grabs a stone and cocks his hand back. Chop holds his breath, and then the woman in red hits the guy with a card.

"I told you those bitches are worth something," Chop says.

James makes it inside and pats the pilot on the back. The chopper goes up.

"How did you get your own chopper?" Bones asks.

"I'm corporate now," James says.

"Hey, I still have more seniority than you," Reeko says.

James looks out as the chopper ascends. The crowd is still dodging the droid.

"How'd you get her to do that?" James asks.

"It's the mustache. Ladies love it," Chop says, curling it.

"What's happening? Turbine problem?" Reeko asks.

"Shield problem," James replies.

Chop starts laughing.

"What's so funny?" Reeko says.

"We got out of there without paying the bill."

The chopper thrusts forward, pushing the guys back into their seats.

15

Fire blasts the silver suit. Inside, the test dummy still has a smile on its face. The heat pours back onto Melissa, Philip, and the observing scientists.

The blast ends. One of the scientists uses a fire extinguisher to spray the suit. Once the smoke clears, there's a black char left on the suits. The glass is cracked an inch, but the test dummy is still smiling.

Melissa looks at the scientists.

"Almost there," the young female scientist says. "Just some adjustments to the thermal core."

Melissa nods. "I know you can do it. Don't be afraid to think outside the box."

The scientists scurry to the suit.

Philip leans in toward Melissa. "Ma'am, the crew has been briefed. They are waiting for you in the blue conference room."

"What do you think?" Melissa asks, leading the way down the corridor.

"These are the guys we saw fixing the turbines in quadrant four yesterday."

"And?" Melissa goes.

"My observation from yesterday still stands. They're a bunch of pigs."

Melissa looks into the conference room. Chop is unwrapping mints on the table. Reeko and James are looking at a smart tablet. Bones is sleeping.

"What did I tell you?" Philip whispers.

Melissa walks in. Reeko pushes Bones to wake him. The four men stand up.

"Gentlemen, please sit," Melissa says as she takes a seat.

Philip sits behind her.

"So you know the situation. You've had time to think. Can this be done?"

Reeko raises his hand a few inches. "Ma'am, I've been working for you for fifteen years. I started on the outside, before the new UVASUITs were required. I started by building and reinforcing those shields. I put my time in, got promoted to repair tech three, and then I wanted to go the supervisor route, but I'm still waiting for that opportunity."

"Okay, *Reeko*," Melissa says, glancing at his name on his uniform. She has a picture of the four men on her smart tablet. "I've checked all your profiles. Reeko, you've got decent annual reviews, but there was an incident five years ago over drunkenness at work."

"Ma'am. I wrote a rebuttal to that. I was off the clock. My supervisor was a dick." Reeko looks at Philip.

"And we have fighting at work, Mr. Bones," Melissa says as she looks at Bones' profile. "And we have frequent tardiness," she says to Chop.

"The mustache is slow to rise in the morning."

"Ma'am," James says. "I've worked alongside these guys for what, eight years now? I would take a bullet for them. They are my family, just as Janice and Brian are. I know they have my back, just as I have theirs."

Melissa looks at her smart tablet. "Well, you guys do have the number one repair rate for turbines."

"That's because of that man over there," Reeko says, gesturing at James.

"That's right," Bones says.

"He's my brother," Chop adds, patting James' back.

Reeko shadow-punches his arm. "I've never worked with anyone with such talent. This man can fix, can engineer, can improvise, can bubble-gum almost anything related to a shield and ventilation system. I wish you could clone him and send four of him up there. But we all stick together, and together we will do what we have to do."

Melissa exhales. She studies James, his blushing cheeks, his humble eyes. She can see his son in his eyes, and in his son, she can see hers. "So, gentlemen, I take it that you are volunteering for this."

"Volunteering?" Bones says. "We're not volunteering. We want to get paid."

"Hell yeah," Chop says.

Melissa glances at Philip, who shakes his head.

"What do you guys want in exchange for your services?" Melissa asks.

Chop and Bones look at Reeko.

"Well, ma'am," Reeko says. "First and foremost, we want to be saved, but we don't just want to be saved, we want to be treated like royalty. Like how they used to in England with those kings and princes. And we would like one of those fancy UVAHOMES and a full pension plan the day we return."

Chop clears his throat. "And I have a special request of one of those new sexy droids with the realistic skin that is so soft and warm, like warm silk in your hands," he says, caressing the air.

"The stuff you want to do with that machine should be illegal," Bones says. "I want a bottle of Jack Daniel's. The *real* stuff."

"Are these guys serious? We should interview other crews," Philip whispers into her ear.

"Do you have families?" Melissa asks.

"I wish I still had a family," Reeko says, lowering his head.

"James is our only family man on the team," Bones says.

"James, you've been quiet ever since you've arrived," Melissa says. "Is there anything special that you want?"

"I just want to save my family."

"Amen, brother," Chop says.

"Now, what are you going to provide us?" Reeko says. "Harvesting steel and reinforcing shields is a textbook job, the stuff I used to do as a rookie. What are we looking at here?"

Melissa stands up and nods at Philip. He goes to load up an image on the screen.

"Gentlemen, I know we discussed the need for your services, but we cannot glance over the fact that this mission is one of a kind. *We are it.* The people here in America are all who are left of this world. The last time we communicated with someone was nine years ago in the dome in Russia. But the heat found its way through their shields and stole the lives of those people, the *last* people. The heat wants to get us down here, and the heat will want to get you up there. You'll be on its playing field."

On the screen, Philip shows a video of fire burning in the sky. Then the video changes to the three scientists walking slowly with their suits.

"Getting to the bridge will take you four hours, harvesting and integration will take you another four, and then the return will take another four hours. We're looking at a full twelve-hour day out there, and then you'll be back to safety. In full disclosure, in the past five years, no one has ever stayed more than four hours on the surface. R&D is working around the clock to create the state-of-the-art next generation UVASUITs, as well as a motorized Rover to get you there."

The video shows the burning eyes of the scorched man under the tractor-trailer.

"What the hell is that?" Bones says.

"We don't know. It could be a camera trick."

Bones sits forward. "That's no camera trick."

Melissa shrugs. "We don't know."

The video shows the panicking freshman scientist with her suit igniting into fire. The other scientist sprays an extinguisher.

"Okay, Philip. That's enough."

Philip turns off the video.

"So, let me get this straight," Reeko says. "You want us to go outside in some Mickey Mouse suits, ride this scooter around, work nonstop, all while there could be some mutants out there ready to pounce on us?"

Melissa exhales. "You will have the support of the best minds in the world."

"In the world?" Bones says. "There're no minds left."

Chop scratches his head. "Yeah, I don't know about all this."

"Guys," James says. "I thought this sounded crazy too. In fact, after I heard the news, I ran away." He looks at Melissa and nods. "But I'm not going to just hide down here and die. No way. I'm going to use my skills to beat this heat. Remember that time last year, when we had four turbines go down within an hour? We were up there working in a hundred and twenty degree heat. We didn't have supplies. Budget cuts were killing us. But I remember what you said, Chop."

Chop sits up.

"You said that working makes you forget about the constant desires of what the world used to be—the beaches, the food, the blue skies."

"The women," Chop says with his eyes closed.

"Working makes me feel like I have a purpose. Working makes me feel like I have a chance to provide a future for my son. He's never going to be able to go to a real beach, never going to be able to eat a steak cooked medium-well smothered with some A.1. Steak Sauce. He's never going to be able to see the blue skies. These are all things that *we've* done before. So I want to keep working, but the difference now is that we have the support of everyone."

James stands up. "I'm in, ma'am."

Chop stands up and joins him. "You can count on me."

Reeko stands up. "I'm ready."

Bones looks around, and then stands up. "Well, that bottle of Jack Daniel's is going to taste good."

Melissa looks into James' eyes and gives him a nod of confidence.

16

The metal on the machine gun reflects the overhead light. The military man stands tall, squeezing his weapon.

Melissa follows Ross toward the entryway as Philip follows her. Gripping his weapon just as tightly, Lance stands at the chopper with his eyes locked with those of the military man.

As Melissa approaches the entrance, she sees the two-bar insignia on the military man's camouflage. He looks into her eyes, steals her breath, and constricts her soul. She looks down, still walking. Suddenly, her briefcase falls to the floor.

Philip picks it up.

"Thank you," she says, coughing.

"Right this way," Ross says, walking them past another guard at the entryway.

Melissa slows down.

"Are you okay, Mrs. Mercer?" Philip says. "Do you need a break?"

"No, I'll be fine."

"The president will be ready in three minutes," the voice in Ross' walkie-talkie says.

Melissa starts coughing.

"Mrs. Mercer, can I get you something?" Philip asks.

"I just need to use the restroom."

"Our restrooms are down there and to the right," Ross says, pointing.

Melissa's stomach turns as sweat covers the back of her neck. Leaving the briefcase, she hustles down the hall. The air becomes hotter. The hallway closes in on her. Melissa makes it to the end and pours into the first door on her right.

Five stalls greet her. She punches open the second stall and hurls up her stomach into the toilet.

After her stomach surrenders, she flushes the toilet and puts the seat down. Then she sits down, basking in the quiet. The hum of a distant turbine pacifies her. She closes her eyes and sees her son and her husband. She's sitting on her bed. Alex is crawling through Richard's legs. Her husband playfully grabs their son. Alex giggles without a care in the world.

Melissa's breathing slows and the sweat on her neck evaporates.

The bathroom door opens.

"In here?" a male voice says.

Melissa opens her eyes. She lifts her legs up and puts them on the toilet seat as her face flushes.

"Yeah," the second male voice says.

Both men saunter inside and move past the stall. Through the seam, she sees the camouflage fatigues of one man and the black suit of another.

"This is the only place without cameras and mics in this whole compound," the second male voice says.

Melissa squints her eyes because she's heard this voice before.

She looks through the seams and sees the slicked gray hair, the wrinkled face, the potbelly, of Secretary Dunner. The other man is the military man from the entryway.

"Are we clear?" Secretary Dunner says.

The military man bends down and looks under the stalls. Melissa pulls her legs to her chest tightly and freezes.

"We're clear, sir," the military man replies.

"Good," the secretary says. "So, do you think we can help each other?"

"My neck's going on the line here."

"Don't worry. You'll be promoted right to the top."

"I need a number."

"Relax. I'm a man of my word," the secretary says. "You have my assurance that you and your family will be saved."

The secretary flushes the urinal, followed by the military man.

Melissa's throat tingles, a cough imminent.

Both men wash their hands and step toward the door.

"Let's go. I don't want anyone to think we're a couple of fags," the secretary says as they both exit.

Melissa exhales and coughs. She steps out from the stall and looks at her face in the mirror. Her skin is pale. Her eyes are red. Her hair is flat. She takes a napkin and wipes her brow.

As she steps to the door, she stops and listens to the sound of silence. Then she pushes the door an inch and sees the deserted hallway.

Outside, Melissa notices the sign next to the door that reads, "Men." The door across from her has a sign marked, "Women." She moves down the corridor.

"I caught you," Secretary Dunner says from behind.

Melissa holds her breath, stopping cold.

"Where's your escort?" the secretary continues.

Melissa turns around. "He's down the hall. I just had to make a pit stop."

"You know, Melissa. I always admired a good businessperson. Hell, I started in business myself. But now that I'm working for the government, part of my job is to defend what's left of this nation from corruption."

Melissa narrows her eyes. "What are you trying to say?"

"Mrs. Mercer, hurry," Ross says.

"You know what I'm trying to say," Secretary Dunner continues, fire in his eyes.

"I'm late for the meeting," Melissa says, moving down the hallway.

"Don't worry, they won't start without me."

Melissa joins Ross and Philip.

"Are you okay, ma'am?" Philip asks.

"Let's do this," she says.

They enter the conference room. The familiar scientists are sitting at their respective spots at the conference table. Philip helps Melissa with the chair and removes the smart tablet from the briefcase. Ross assumes his position in the middle of the room.

The president steps out, the part in his hair crooked, his suit full of wrinkles. Everyone stands up. Secretary Dunner follows him, staring at Melissa's soul.

"Okay, everyone," the president says. "Be seated."

Everyone sits down except the president.

"Who the hell is the mole?" the president says.

Melissa holds her breath. The room remains mute.

"My office is getting calls from every news organization down here. People are getting restless. Someone's leaking information. I know you're all fearful of the future. But we have to remain strong." The president sits down. "Mrs. Mercer, I hope you've selected the best and the most qualified individuals for us."

Ross presses a button. The screen turns on and shows James, Chop, Bones, and Reeko sitting inside the conference room at UVASHIELD. Chop is fixing his mustache. Bones is slouched in his chair. Reeko is clenching his fist. James is staring blankly into the lens.

Secretary Dunner chuckles and shakes his head.

"This is the best you got?" the president says. "Can they hear me?"

The four guys sit up.

"Yes, sir," Reeko says. "We're all here."

"Sir," Melissa says, getting the attention of the room. "As you have said, we're all under stress here. I assure you that this team is my best crew. I've spoken with them. They are all on board. They know the severity of this situation. But they do have a list of requests." Melissa hands Ross a sheet of paper, who then delivers it to the president.

"Who are you all?" the president asks.

"Reeko, sir. Tech level three. Welding."

"Bones, sir. Tech level two. Lubrication and Maintenance."

"I'm Chop, sir. Tech level three. Mechanical."

Secretary Dunner shakes his head.

"And I am James, sir. James Wilson. We met earlier. I'm Tech level four. Electrical."

"What is this?" The president says as he puts on his glasses to read the list. "Simulated women? Jack Daniel's?"

Secretary Dunner grabs the list.

"Mrs. Mercer," the president says. "I trust your judgment, but please, be honest with me. I'm about to go on the smart screen network to address the nation."

"Yes, sir. These men are our best."

The president takes off his glasses. "Men, I will ensure your requests are satisfied. You are all about to be famous whether you like it or not. I ask that you stay professional and that you listen to direction, and above all, that you give one hundred percent on this job. There are no second chances. Do you each understand that?"

The four men collectively say, "Yes, sir."

"I want everyone to look at the clock on our screen. Do you see that? Five days, fifteen hours, fifty-three minutes."

"Uh, about the clock," Secretary Dunner says.

"Not now," the president replies. He looks at Melissa. "When are we going to be ready for action?"

"Sir, our new UVASUITs are almost ready," Melissa says. "I would estimate a matter of days. Our crew will be ready very shortly."

"*Very shortly* or a *matter of days* won't cut it, Mrs. Mercer. We don't have time to estimate."

"I need to speak," Secretary Dunner says.

"Go ahead," the president says.

"They must be ready by tomorrow. Our scientists are seeing the temperatures rise even further. I thought you would know this, Mrs. Mercer." Secretary Dunner looks at the female scientist at the table.

She sits up. "Yes. Our team, including members of your staff, Mrs. Mercer, are seeing the spikes occurring more frequently. I would advise that this gets accomplished as soon as possible."

"Sir, I think we should question whether Mrs. Mercer can handle the pressure," Secretary Dunner says.

"That's enough," the president says. He looks at the female scientist at the table. "What are you saying?"

"Sir, our timeline has just shrunk." The female scientist nods at Ross, who clicks a button.

On the screen, "5 days" changes to "2 days."

Gasps come from the corners of the room.

Melissa leans toward Philip. "Why wasn't I aware of this first?"

"Ma'am, there was a lot of activity going on when you fainted. Someone updated these slides. I couldn't keep a handle on it all."

Chop whispers to the table, "What did we get ourselves into?"

The president rubs his eyebrows and exhales, "This is not happening."

"It *is* happening," Secretary Dunner says.

The president sits up.

"Mrs. Mercer," Secretary Dunner continues. "You have fourteen hours. Your suits, your staff, everything must be vetted, must be fully operational within this time."

"Will your team be ready by tomorrow? Seven a.m.?" the president asks Melissa.

She clears her throat. "They will need to start training a.s.a.p."

"We will be ready, sir," James says.

The clock on the screen shows, "2 days, 15 hours, 49 minutes, 25 seconds"... "24 seconds"...

17

Corn boils in a pot.

A cook wearing an apron stirs it. "Corn! Get some real corn!"

Hundreds of people roam through the underbelly of quadrant four. Drunks pour out of Hot Henry's Bar. A woman in a red dress hands out cards. A security officer wearing black roves through the crowd.

People gather around the vendor.

The cook dumps the corn into a strainer, removing the water. He fills tiny paper cups with corn. "Freshly boiled corn here! That's right, we have *real* corn today!"

"How much?" a woman asks.

"Only one hundred credits."

"That's ridiculous!" she says.

"It's real corn, grown in the greenhouse. Boiled fresh just like grandma used to make."

Another woman hands him a credit card. The cook taps it against a checkout machine. A beep registers. He gives the lady back her card and hands her one of the tiny cups.

She swallows the contents in one gulp.

"Good, huh?" the cook says.

She smiles, corn stuck in her teeth.

"Want more?"

"That's a day's salary I just gave you," she says.

"Was it worth it?"

She licks the contents of the cup. "Worth every credit."

"Corn! Get your corn here!" the cook shouts, filling more cups.

A chubby man offers his credit card. "I'll take two."

Suddenly, a hobo in a ripped T-shirt grabs a cup.

The cook runs after him. "Thief!"

When he leaves his stand, three more hobos snatch the pot of corn.

"Security!" the cook shouts at the security officer twenty yards away in the crowd.

"Attention citizens of the United States of America," fills the entire underground space.

The hobo freezes. The cook stops chasing him. The security officer turns to the screen. The people in the crowd stop walking, stop talking, stop stalking.

Capturing the attention of the crowd, the image of President Brooks projects onto the twenty-foot screen overhead. He sits behind a desk, the seal of the president over his shoulder, a picture of him with his wife, son, and daughter framed on the stand behind him.

He addresses the crowd, "My fellow Americans. Wherever you are right now in this new nation of ours, I ask for your attention. Since Underground Day on August twenty-fourth, twenty twenty-five, we have all been forced to develop a new America. I'm sure our Founding Fathers had never envisioned the world in which we live today. But America is strong, declaring freedom from the British, winning two World Wars, securing equal rights for women and minorities. Today, it doesn't matter your skin color, your age, your gender. We're all in this together, and we're all who are left in the world. And just as America is strong, powerful, and smart, a new challenge faces us. As you know, the world that we live in down here, the new America, can only sustain our way of life via a complex system of shielding components and air-quality turbines. It has been very difficult over the years to collect data to understand the composition of the world above us and to model the effects of the extreme temperatures on our ability to survive in our new America. Thirty-six hours ago, top scientists in the government and the private sector have discovered something alarming in the temperature of the outside world. It started with a routine data collection mission of the outside that ended in the death of a young scientist, Miss Rachel Banks. Our thoughts and our prayers are with Miss Banks and her family. After this incident, top scientists have discovered that the models we used to determine our ability to survive down here were wrong, *very* wrong. I wish I had some magic solution to fix this Earth, but I am like you, relying on our shielding and ventilation systems to survive. Miss Banks' death was not in vain, as this incident prompted us to discover the truth of the situation—the temperatures are exponentially rising and will overtake our shields' ability to function in…two days from now."

People gasp in the crowd. A gray-haired man swallows hard. A boy squeezes his father's hand. A woman digs her nails into her forearm.

"While this challenge faces us, America is not afraid. We have tackled dozens of problems in our past, and have conquered all of them. UVASHIELD, the company who engineers and maintains these complex systems, has assembled a team of their very best crew members."

A picture of James, Chop, Bones, and Reeko fills the top corner of the screen.

"This team has some of the most advanced training from UVASHIELD and they have a combined total of forty-three years working on our ventilation systems. The mission of this team will be to reinforce the shielding systems with hardened steel harvested from the Ben Franklin Bridge. Special UVASUITs and other specialized tools are being finalized and tested to ensure a safe and successful mission."

The camera moves in tight on the president as his eyes grow heavy. "Now, there is also unforgiving news." He exhales.

The cook holds his breath. The hobos stop chewing the corn.

"I wish I didn't have to say what I'm about to say. We…we can only save one thousand individuals."

Shrieks and gasps erupt from the crowd.

"The only fair way to do this is by lottery. According to our census bureau, we have ninety-nine thousand three hundred forty-five Americans. So this means that ninety-*eight* thousand three hundred forty-five will not be selected. What does this mean for these Americans? It means that you will forever be honored, forever be a part of the survivors after Underground Day, forever be Americans." The president chokes up.

The crowd boos. The gray-haired man spits on the ground. The boy lets go of his father's hand. The woman licks the smudges of blood on her fingers.

"The details of this lottery will be forthcoming, but we will select randomly based on your social security numbers. For those of you who do not have social security numbers, we will have a process to include you. There are many variables in this news, many paths that America can take. Thank you for listening, my fellow Americans. And may God have mercy on us all."

The screen goes black. People scream. Chaos ensues.

Suddenly, two helicopters fly in with "U.S. Army" scrawled across their sides. Men in fatigues slide down ropes. "Attention citizens. The United States Army is enacting martial law. All citizens must return to their residences to await further instructions."

People throw trash at the helicopters. The woman in the red dress falls into the crowd. Someone steps on her head, cracking it open. Wires pour out.

The cook sees three burly guys topple over his vending cart. The hobos scoop the corn up from the ground and put it back into the pot.

The cook goes down. Feet step around him, on him. He tries to stand, but the crowd is too much.

As he lies on the ground, a single piece of corn rolls toward him. It's so plump. Its yellow color is so intense. A tear slides down his cheek. "Just like grandma used to make," he whispers as a boot crushes his skull.

18

An oversized golf cart creeps around a cone. The tires turn slightly, the side of the vehicle inching closer to the cone.

"Slower!" Reeko shouts.

The Rover keeps crawling, but then rockets forward and squashes the cone.

"Goddamn! Where'd you learn to drive?" Reeko says.

Dressed in tan UVASUITs, the crew is sitting inside the Rover. Bones is driving. Reeko is next to him with James and Chop on the rear bench seat. The Rover is two feet longer than a golf cart and three feet wider. It has truck-sized tires with deep tread. The metal is polished black with the UVASHIELD logo proudly displayed on both sides. In the rear behind Chop and James, ports from two mini jet-propulsion engines expel exhaust.

Two scientists watch with clipboards.

"This throttle is messed up," Bones says. "There's too much play."

All the guys jump off as the scientists jump on and check the wires under the dash.

James goes over to a workbench and picks up a hammer and screwdriver.

"What do you think?" Chop asks.

James moves his hands around. "Not bad. The joints in the suit move right with your hands."

"I don't know," Chop says, picking up a bucket. "I feel like I'm in a big condom."

"Going out there without protection is like banging a cheap hooker on steroids," Reeko says.

"You idiots need to look at the positives," Bones says. "This suit has a liquid tank, like one of those beer hats they used to sell. Remember those? You'd have the straw right in the top."

They all laugh.

"I like the heads-up display," James says. An overlay of stats displays in the view out from his helmet. There are vitals that read, "Oxygen Level: 99%, Internal Temperature: 73, External Temperature: 80."

"How does it work?" Chop asks.

"Just use your eyes," James says. "Focus and stare at the menu item to select it."

Bones stares at the word *Hydration* in the corner of his heads-up display. It flashes and shows, "Hydration Container 1: 100%, Hydration Container 2: Empty." He selects "Hydration Container 1." A straw lowers in the suit. "Hey, this is cool!"

Chop blinks his eyes. "This is going to make me go senile."

"You're already senile," Reeko says.

Bones starts blowing into the straw, which makes a bubbling sound. "Hey! Sounds like my old bong!"

"Take those suits off now!" Philip says, walking into the lab.

"Can you pull down my zipper, handsome?" Chop says with a high-pitched voice.

Bones and Reeko laugh. James chuckles.

Philip shakes his head. "We need each of you to meet with a psychologist."

"A shrink? What is this?" Reeko says.

"It's just standard procedure," Philip replies.

The guys remove the suits and place them back in their holding bays. As they follow Philip, they pass the testing chamber with the four new silver suits. Two scientists are loading the test dummies into them.

Bones runs over. "Wait, you forgot the most important part." He grabs a marker from the table and draws a curlicue mustache on one of the test dummies.

"It's thicker than that," Chop goes.

Bones traces it again, making it darker.

"Come on, boys," Philip says. "We have a very tight schedule."

"If that mustache is burned off, I'm not wearing that condom," Chop shouts.

Philip squints his eyes as he leads the guys toward four individual conference rooms. Four psychologists—two men, two women—stand holding smart tablets and sporting blank expressions. Each psychologist takes a man into his or her respective room.

Back in the lab, a buzzer sounds and a red light flashes. A fireball attacks the suits.

After thirty seconds, the fire stops. The suits have only minor charring. The test dummy inside the second suit still has his curlicue mustache.

Inside room one, Reeko is sitting at the table with his arms crossed.

"So tell me about your love life," the male psychologist asks.

"I like women, *man*," Reeko replies.

"Why do you call your coworkers using a female term such as *ladies*, *girls*, or *bitches*?"

"What does this have to do with fixing a shield?"

"Answer the questions in any way you choose," the psychologist says.

Reeko cracks his knuckles. "How about you ask me what size a 9mm socket is closest to in the English system?"

In room two, Bones is slouched down in a chair, the female psychologist across from him.

"It says that you have come to work under the influence of alcohol at least three times over the past year." She looks at Bones. "Do you have a drinking problem?"

"Of course I have a drinking problem. My problem is I don't make enough credits to buy the top-shelf liquor."

In the third room, Chop is crying. "I loved her, man. She was so beautiful."

The male psychologist writes in his smart tablet, "Relationship issues."

"What did you do after this droid rejected you at the brothel?"

"I started growing this mustache and I haven't stopped since."

"Would you ever consider shaving it off?"

Chop stops crying. He sits up and says in a deep voice, "No one messes with this mustache."

In the fourth room, James is sitting with his hands resting on the table.

The female psychologist looks at his work history in the smart tablet. "Twelve years with UVASHIELD, excellent attendance records, started at technician level one and promoted in twenty thirty-six, twenty forty, and twenty forty-four. Why didn't you want to go the management route?"

"I love fixing things. Ever since I was a kid, I liked building and fixing computers and gadgets."

She smiles and writes, "Hard worker."

"So, you're the only family man in the group," she says.

"That's right."

"Your son is…"

"He's nine," James says, smiling. "He's such a smart kid. He loves building models."

"How is your relationship with your wife?"

James pauses, warmth fills his eyes as the image of Janice in her wedding dress floats in front of him, her hair long and curled, her eyes accented by blue eye shadow. "Aww, she's the love of my life."

"When did you meet her?"

"We met down here after Underground Day. I was living alone and working temp jobs back then. I took a cooking class. That's where we met."

"Any regrets getting married?"

James chuckles. "It was the best decision I ever made. I guess I only regret not having credits for a bigger wedding. I wish I could've danced with her in front of our families."

The psychologist smiles and writes, "Good family life."

"How about your parents?"

"Oh, my parents." James looks down and sees the horror in their faces as the Earth swallows them. "They passed away. During the big earthquake."

"I'm sorry to hear that. How did you make it down here during Underground Day?"

"Well, I was in one of the refugee camps near Philadelphia. I was fifteen when the doors opened for that one day." James shakes his head, his eyes staring at a divot in the wood on the table. "I guess I was just at the right place at the right time to make it underground."

She remains mute and writes, "Fears?"

"Well, this all seems fine. How do you feel about the task at hand? There's a lot of pressure on your shoulders."

James looks at her. "The job is cake. I started out there building and reinforcing the shields when it wasn't as bad."

"A lot has changed up there since that time," the psychologist says.

"I know, but I have a great team and great support from everyone. Mrs. Mercer has been so reassuring that the suits will be ready and that her best scientists will be assisting us. Heck, the president even confided his support. I'm fine. I'm just looking forward to getting done and getting back to my family."

"So you will be part of the one thousand who will be saved?"

James looks into her eyes and sees a quiver of fear. "Oh, I'm sorry. I didn't mean to sound arrogant. I know there are a lot of us that we cannot save."

"No, it's fine. You and your family should certainly be saved for your sacrifice."

She writes in her tablet, "Humble."

She exhales and looks at James. "We're just about done here. I know you have a lot to do, but I do have one more question."

"Sure."

She looks deep inside his eyes. "What do you fear?"

James holds his breath. The way she says the word *fear*, the inflection in her voice, the emphasis of the single syllable, rattles inside his brain and removes him from the room. He's back again as a boy on the ground. He feels the Earth shaking and sees the hole open in front of him. His parents are in the stands. His mother screams. His father looks through the chaos and connects eyes with him, his only child. James goes to them, but the Earth opens its mouth and swallows his parents.

"James?" the psychologist says.

"What?"

"You didn't answer my question. What do you fear?"

"I fear no one," he says, standing up.

"That's not the question I asked. *What* do you fear? It could be the fear of heights, the fear of the cold, the fear of—"

"Dying," he whispers.

A knock sounds at the door. Philip peeks inside. "Sorry for interrupting. Your family is safe and has been rerouted to our secure quarters, Mr. Wilson."

"I'm finished here, right?" James says to the psychologist.

In her smart tablet, she circles the word *Fear*, and then she stands up. "Uh, yes, I think we are all wrapped up."

"Thank you, ma'am," James says, shaking her hand.

"Good luck, James. Do your best. Be with your family now."

James steps out, leaving the psychologist alone inside the empty room.

She takes a deep breath and whispers, "I'm afraid of dying too."

19

Stars shine in the sky. Crickets chirp. The scent of the moist summer air swirls. A shooting star races across the night. Suddenly, the sky flickers into a flat white ceiling.

"Alex!" Richard shouts.

Alex is sitting on the couch, admiring the simulated night sky.

Richard opens the door and turns on the lights. "There you are. I told you to get your stuff packed. Only the essentials. Your mom is coming to get us."

"I'm going to miss this thing."

Richard steps in. "I'm going to miss a lot of our things too. But we'll get new stuff. Our lives are the most important thing."

"I know, but what's going to happen to us? What about the kids in school?"

Richard flips the light switch off. "Put the night simulation back on."

Alex presses some buttons on the remote. The starry sky comes back.

Richard sits down on the couch and takes a deep breath. "Aww, it smells so fresh."

"Would you do this before Underground Day?"

"Yeah. I would, with Mom. Before you were born, before all this down here, even before Underground Day and the big quake, your mom and I would sit outside in the summer at my parents' house in the Pocono Mountains."

"Where are the Pocono Mountains?" Alex asks.

"They are about a hundred miles north. The air was so clean there. The summer nights were warm. The stars were so bright. The sounds of the night would surround you."

They remain silent for a moment listening to the crickets sing.

"Where did you meet Mom?" Alex asks.

"She moved down the street from my house in Mountain Top in our senior year of high school. The school was small and we knew everyone in our class, kind of like how you know everyone in your class. After we graduated, she went to University of Pennsylvania and I went to Penn State, but we stayed together. And those summers when your mom and I were home from college, we would just sit out at night and gaze up at the universe."

"It sounds nice."

"It was, buddy." He holds his son tightly. "But your generation has imaginations that far exceed anything that your mom and I have. Your mind has no limit."

The room starts shaking, the image flickering from the night sky to the white ceiling.

"What's going on?" Alex says.

"I don't know. Let's just get ready."

They hear the front door open. Melissa walks in. "What are you two doing? I told you to get ready. I have the transport here. They will take us to our facility where it'll be safer."

"Safer from what?" Richard says.

More shaking occurs. The lights flicker again.

"After the president's announcement, disorder is in the air."

Richard sees Melissa's face, which is pale and sweaty. "What's wrong? You look so weak."

"I'm busy," she says. "I haven't had any time to lie under the Sim-Sun."

"Go get your stuff, Alex," Richard says.

Alex scurries into his room.

Richard moves to Melissa and embraces her, smelling her salty scent. "Honey, you should get checked out. You fainted before. You've got to take care of your health."

"I've got to take care of the world. The team is almost ready. The suits are almost done. There's something going on with the president and his cabinet. I overheard Secretary Dunner in the men's room talking in private to a military officer."

"In the men's bathroom? What were you doing in there?"

"I had to vomit."

"Honey, we're calling the doctor right now."

She breaks the embrace. "There's no time. Just get your stuff. I'll be fine. Let's go." Melissa moves past him to the kitchen. "Where're those gold coins we have?"

Richard shrugs and scratches his beard.

Five minutes later, Melissa, Richard, and Alex hustle from their home, suitcases rolling at their sides. Richard slides his fingerprint across a scanner; the door locks. They move down a corridor lined with doors.

One of them opens and an elderly woman steps out wearing a bathrobe and holding a RoboDog. "Oh, Melissa. There you are."

The family slows down.

"I hate to bother you, dear," the elderly woman says. "But can you get me a lottery ticket?"

"I wish I could get one for everyone," Melissa replies.

The woman starts crying.

Melissa stops, causing Alex and Richard to stop as well. She puts her arms around her. "I'm so sorry, Mrs. Walton. Just sit tight in your home. They will announce the numbers soon."

The woman looks down at Alex and smiles. "You have a wonderful son, Melissa."

Melissa smiles as she leads the way down the corridor. As they exit into an open area, the sound of a chopper buzzes. Her helicopter is waiting, the pilot ready to take off.

"We're going on a helicopter ride," Melissa says.

"Cool!" Alex says.

Richard goes over.

Lance slides open the door and helps Alex and his father inside with their suitcases.

"There she is!" a male voice shouts.

An angry guy is leading a group of five others with bats and crowbars clutched in their hands. "She has the tickets! Stop her!"

Lance waves her over with his pistol. "Hurry, ma'am!"

Melissa hustles toward the open door, but the sound of the chopper fades. The spinning blades hypnotize her, spinning and spinning and spinning.

"Ma'am, let's go!" Lance yells.

"Melissa! Hurry!" Richard shouts.

She falls down to one knee, her suitcase dropping. The angry guy storms toward her and raises his bat.

Lance dives through the air, losing his pistol, and tackles the guy.

Richard rushes out and grabs his wife.

She reaches for her suitcase, three feet from the angry guy.

"Just leave it!" Richard says.

With half-open eyes, Melissa stumbles toward the chopper.

"Mom!" Alex yells.

"Get back!" Lance shouts, pushing back the mob. He runs to Melissa and helps her in, her leg dangling off the side.

People crack open Melissa's suitcase and toss clothes aside. Gold coins roll everywhere. People push and shove, grabbing coins. A woman with blood on her hands rips apart a picture of the Mercer family.

"Go! Just go!" Richard shouts to the pilot when Lance tumbles in.

The chopper lifts up. Someone in the mob swings a crowbar, busting a sensor on the belly of the chopper, sending it bobbling.

"Stop them!" the angry guy yells, grabbing Lance's pistol.

The chopper goes up. Richard and Alex pull Melissa inside as Lance catches a stone in mid-air.

The angry guy shoots; bullets ricochet off the door of the chopper.

Alex shrieks.

Lance chucks the rock at the angry guy, hitting his arm, which causes him to drop the gun. "Go! Go! Go!"

"Mom! Mom!" Alex shouts.

"Honey, look at me," Richard says, looking into Melissa's lost eyes.

She sees the face of her husband, the face of her son, but their words are muffled, as if they are underwater. She focuses on the spinning blades outside, spinning and spinning and spinning.

"Go to the hospital!" Richard shouts.

"The hospitals are overrun," the pilot says.

"She needs help!"

"We have a medical facility at UVASHIELD."

"Okay. Fly. Fast," Richard says.

Alex cradles his mom's head, stroking her hair. He puts his hand on her head and feels the heat radiating from her. "I love you, Mom."

20

A military man grips an assault rifle. Brian adjusts the six-inch action figure on an end table. He grabs two more military men from the cot and points their guns at the UVASHIELD logo on the wall while simulating the sound of machine guns with his voice. Then he points them at the suitcase on top of the other cot.

The door to the room opens. Brian points the action figures at the door as Janice walks in.

"Brian, stop that!" she says.

He sits down on the cot.

"Are you unpacked?" she asks, unzipping her suitcase.

"Yeah, but I want to go home."

"Well, like we already talked about, we can't go back to our home. That's in a quadrant that will soon be too hot to live in."

"I don't like it in this room. It's so small. How long do we have to stay here?"

"Until your dad finishes his job."

"I wish we could go back to our home."

"I thought you said it was too small."

"It is, but it's our home."

Janice hangs up some blouses in the closet. "When I was your age, I moved around a lot. It's normal to move. As long as we're together."

"Why does Dad have to work?" Brian says. "I heard some people saying that he's going on a suicide mission. What is *suicide*?"

Janice misses the bar and drops clothes onto the floor.

James opens the door.

"Dad!" Brian shouts, running to him.

They embrace.

"You made it," James says. "How was the chopper ride?"

"It was *so* cool! We flew so fast and were turning down the corridors, but the ride was so smooth. And then we flew over the people in the common area. There were army guys all around and people were throwing stuff at us. We had to dodge it all. It was like a game."

"It was sad," Janice says. "Why do they think we're the enemy?"

"At least you made it safely," James says, kissing his wife.

"Where're you going to sleep, Dad?"

"Well, I'm supposed to leave in eight hours. I'm still training."

James and Janice sit down on the cot, Brian on the floor.

"How's everything going?" Janice asks.

James exhales. "Well, I don't know. We're all just thinking about the task. I hope the suits are ready, but they're working on them. Everyone's working nonstop. Bones is learning to drive the Rover. And we just met with psychologists."

"Psychologists? Why?"

"You know, it's all standard procedure," he says, staring at the drain on the floor.

"What is Melissa saying?" Janice asks.

"What?" he says.

"Melissa. What is she saying?"

"I haven't seen her in a few hours. I think she's getting her family and had meetings with the president."

"Are you sure you're okay?" Janice says, rubbing his leg.

"Yeah. Don't worry. I know these shield systems inside and out. The only difference is that we're going to be working outside in these new suits."

"What's up there?" Brian asks. "Are there people?"

"No, tiger. The outside world is too hot for anyone to live."

"Someone said there are monsters up there?" Janice says.

"Monsters!" Brian shouts.

James sits up. "No, there are no monsters. Just something that looked like a person in a video they took."

"You said there were no people," Brian says.

"Well, it wasn't a person."

Brian's stomach twists. "So, they *are* monsters."

"No. I think it was just a camera trick."

"I mean, if there are things alive up there, how can they survive in the heat?" Janice asks.

"I don't know. All I know is that we're going to the bridge. The Ben Franklin Bridge, just like your model, tiger. We're going to use its steel to help reinforce the shields."

Brian smiles. "That's so cool, Dad."

The door bursts open. A military man wields a gun. Janice shrieks. James shields his son.

"Who are you? What are you doing in this room?" the soldier says, pointing his gun at James.

"I have clearance. I'm part of the team going to fix the shields."

"Let me see your credentials."

James pulls his badge up from around his neck.

The soldier checks it. "And what about them?"

James reaches into his wallet.

The soldier raises his weapon.

James slows his movements as he removes two badges.

The soldier inspects them.

"They just got here," James says. "I didn't get a chance to give them their badges."

The soldier puts down his weapon. "We're increasing security. All users must show their badges until zero seven hundred hours when the lottery drawing occurs. Then you must have a ticket to be here." The military man raises his weapon and leaves.

"Why is the military here?" Janice says. "I thought there was just UVASHIELD security."

James rubs his temples. "I don't know."

"What about our tickets? We're promised tickets. That's the only reason you agreed to this."

"Just calm down, honey. When Melissa gets here, she will make sure everything is okay."

Brian goes to the military action figures and hides them in his duffel bag.

21

Bold letters form the word *save* in a sentence on the page. Melissa looks up from the book. She's sitting outside the coffee shop, the sun shining in the blue sky, traffic flowing by, people window-shopping on the sidewalk.

The man wheeling the baby carriage is coming down the sidewalk.

Melissa stands up, knocking over her coffee cup, spilling coffee onto the book.

The two young women gasp and clutch their bags from Victoria's Secret. Melissa looks at the gate blocking her way to the sidewalk. She steps over it, knocking over the plate on her table with the turkey sandwich.

She runs to the man. It's Richard. She sees the baby inside, her baby, her Alex.

"Hurry. We have to go!" Melissa shouts.

"What are you talking about?" Richard says.

"Listen. The earthquake is coming. Please, we must escape." She snatches the baby.

"Hey!" Richard yells.

The ground starts shaking. People scream. A car wrecks. Baby Alex starts crying. The taxi races toward the sidewalk.

She turns around to go back to Richard, to save him, but the cab plows into her and takes her baby away. She's pinned underneath the vehicle, legs twisted, pain seizing her body. The sound of baby Alex's cries motivates her to crawl toward the rear of the car.

The pain pulls her, but the cries push her.

As she reaches her baby, she looks up at the blue sky, but the sun burns her eyes.

Suddenly, a face stands over her view. It's Richard. She's looking at the bright bulb of a light from a hospital bed, an IV line running into her left arm.

"Turn down that light," Richard says.

A chubby nurse lowers it.

Alex runs to the bed.

"What happened?" Melissa says, her voice unsteady.

"You fainted again," Richard says.

"What time is it? How long have I been out?"

"About an hour."

The nurse checks her IV.

Melissa goes to sit up. "I have to go see how the suits are doing."

"No, you must rest," Richard says.

"The doctor will be in to give you the results of the tests," the nurse says.

"Tests? What kind of tests?" Melissa says, lying back down.

"A CBC, chem panel, blood gases, chest X-ray, and CT scan of the brain," a deep voice says at the doorway.

The gray-haired doctor steps inside, holding a clipboard.

"Doctor Young, what's going on?" Melissa says. "What do the tests say?"

He stands over her bed. "Well, nothing yet, the lab is backed up. It may take some time until we get the results. How are you feeling?"

"Just a little tired. I'm okay. I have work to do."

"Melissa, I've been the physician on staff for you for what, five years now? I understand the extreme pressure that has been placed onto you. Everyone's body handles this stress differently. Delegate these tasks to your staff. Your health is the most important thing."

"I understand, but none of this stuff will matter if we don't succeed, if *I* don't succeed. I promise to drink more fluids, take some vitamins and energy pills, whatever you have, but please don't ask me to stop, not until this all gets resolved."

The doctor looks at Richard and Alex, and then back at Melissa. "Until we get the results back, I want to give you a banana bag through your IV. This will replenish your electrolytes and provide your body with nutrients. Then you must drink plenty of water, the *real* water from the bedrock, until further notice."

Melissa grips Richard's hand and sits up. "I will, Doctor. How long until I can go check on my staff?"

"Thirty minutes."

Philip runs into the room. "Mrs. Mercer, you're okay. There's not much time, and there's military running around the place checking badges. They assumed control over our own security staff."

A beefy military man storms in, wielding his gun. "Badges, everyone."

"This is my company, my space. Who do you think you are?"

"I have executive orders straight from the Secretary of Defense to ensure everyone is where they should belong. I need to see everyone's badge."

Two younger military men come in and check everyone's ID badge. When they get to Melissa, she looks at the ceiling, frozen.

"Badge, ma'am," one of the younger military men asks, the gun clanking on the plastic of the bed.

Richard grabs the badge from her purse.

"This facility is being locked down," the beefy military man says. "No one leaves unless cleared by the Office of the Secretary of Defense."

The military men leave.

Melissa looks at her son, who has tears in his eyes. "It's okay, baby." She turns to the doctor. "Let's go. I need to get back to work."

22

Fire attacks the four silver suits. After ten seconds, the fire stops. The silver shines with no char marks present. The test dummies inside are still intact. The mustache on one of them is still curling.

The scientists check smart tablets as Melissa observes nearby. Her complexion is pale, her hair greasy, her business suit wrinkled. One of the scientists gives the thumbs up, which makes Melissa crack a smile.

The Rover moves around the course, now with a trailer attached to the rear. With ease, Bones commands it around cones and over simulated rocks.

Inside UVASUITs, Reeko and Chop discharge fire from blowtorches onto three ten-foot steel beams.

James puts socket wrenches, screwdrivers, and bolt cutters into a toolbox as Philip watches him.

Down a corridor, through a kitchen where three chefs are making wafers, and into a small room, Brian and Janice lie in the dark on separate cots, their eyes wide open.

"Mom," Brian says.

"Yes, baby."

"I can't sleep."

"Aww, what's wrong?"

"I keep thinking about Dad."

"Me too," she says. "He's making sure he's ready for his job. Come lay with me."

Brian moves to his mom and nestles against her warm body.

Down another corridor, Alex and Richard lie inside a similar room. Their eyes are open, fixated on the concrete ceiling.

"Are you awake, Dad?" Alex asks.

"Yeah, buddy."

"Do you think Mom is going to be okay?"

"Yeah, I think she is just so busy with everything. She has a very important job."

"I wish we had the screen to look at on the ceiling," Alex says.

"I know, buddy. Let's just be happy that we have a safe place to stay."

Hours later, beyond the confines of UVASHIELD and into quadrant four, doctors and nurses float around a twenty-patient bed ward overfilled with fifty beds. Some people sleep. Others cry, while others beg for a doctor.

A nurse opens a supply cart and grabs a bag of saline. Underneath, there's a ticking clock with wires connecting to a brick.

She holds her breath, but the ticks don't care. The bomb explodes.

Inside UVASHIELD, the floors rattle. James and the other three men stop working in the lab. Melissa looks up from her smart tablet in her office. Janice, Brian, Richard, and Alex all sit up in their respective cots.

A male voice emits on the loudspeakers, "Attention personnel, please proceed to the common area in Laboratory B. I repeat—all personnel, please proceed to the common area in Laboratory B. This is not a drill."

Philip opens the door to Melissa's office as the compound shudders. Melissa clutches the desk, her eyes widening.

Philip hugs the doorframe. "Ma'am, there's a riot in neighboring quadrant four. This shaking is from explosions of military helicopters."

"We're losing it," Melissa says.

"The military wants us all into the common area."

She shakes her head. "Where's Lance?"

"All our personnel are here with their families in our surplus suites. But our security members are not working. The military has relieved them of their duties."

"Everyone to the common area!" a soldier yells from the corridor.

Melissa presses her temples to push away the pain. "I'm losing my company."

In the common area, dozens of people congregate. Kids are in pajamas. Some adults are in T-shirts and robes, while others are in lab coats.

Alex sees Brian in the crowd and runs to him. "Hey!"

"Alex, I didn't know you were here," Brian says.

"Yeah, me and my dad are staying here."

"Me and my mom too."

Janice catches up and sees Richard. "Richard, what's going on?"

"I don't know."

Another jolt shakes the crowd. People gasp. An elderly woman stumbles as two men wearing UVASHIELD security shirts save her from falling.

James searches through the crowd. A baby cries. Twin six-year-olds clutch their mother's hands. A stocky military man storms toward a raised platform in the room.

James moves deeper into the crowd. He sees a pair of tennis shoes, light green with white laces. He knows they're a kids' size four not because of guessing, but because he had purchased them for his son.

He makes eye contact with Brian, and then with Janice standing above him.

"Honey, there you are," she says.

James nods at Richard and Alex.

"What's going on?" James asks.

"We thought you'd know," Janice says.

"Okay! Listen up, everyone!" the stocky military man shouts.

Everyone simmers down.

"The shaking you are feeling is from explosions in quadrant four. Someone or a group of individuals has placed C-4 explosives in various locations, including a hospital. Explosives have also been found near the turbine units in quadrant one. We are under attack!"

The crowd shrieks.

Bones and Reeko join James.

"What the hell is this? We have to leave in an hour," Reeko says, looking at the clock on the wall showing 6:00.

Bones scans the room. "Where the hell is Chop?"

"I thought he was with you," James says.

Reeko widens his eyes. "I thought he was with *you.*"

"The Secretary of Defense has ordered a sweep of the entire area. There are moles amongst us that are creating terror. We do not know the extent of these planted bombs, but we must ensure the area here is safe. You all must stay here until the area has been cleared."

"What?!" comes from the crowd.

Melissa storms to the podium, Philip following her.

"There's mom!" Alex shouts.

The crowd chants, "Mercer! Mercer! Mercer!"

She steps in front of the stocky military man. "Please, everyone. I know you're all scared. I will ensure your safety and your safe working environment. Until I can get a grasp on where we are, I ask that you please stay calm and listen to all military personnel. Stay with your families."

Melissa steps down as the crowd chatters.

Lance moves toward her wearing a black UVASHIELD security polo shirt. "Ma'am, we are standing by," he whispers, gesturing to the bulge on his ankle.

Melissa nods, and then moves toward her family as Philip follows her. She sees Alex clutching his dad's waist.

"At least you're safe," she says, hugging her husband and son. She sees James and his family.

"We have to leave in an hour," Reeko says.

"This is just a bomb scare," Melissa says. "I know my facility is safe."

Philip nods in agreement.

"Where's Chop?" Bones asks.

"He's not here?" Melissa says.

Reeko rolls his shoulders from stiffness. "He was working with us in the lab."

"Was everything okay there?"

"Yeah," Reeko says. "We had our packs ready. Bones got the driving down. Then the shaking."

"I thought it was an earthquake, Mom," Alex says.

Melissa holds her breath. She moves closer to her husband and son and holds on to them.

Someone's pocket beeps. James pulls out his smart phone and sees, "One New Message." He opens it: "Help! In back of Rover. Phone ready to die. –Chop."

"It's Chop," James says.

"Where is he?" Bones asks.

"He's in the back of the Rover. He needs help."

"Shit," Reeko goes.

"I need to go get him," James says.

Janice squeezes his arm. "No, you're staying here with us."

"Yeah, man," Reeko says. "You stay here with your family. Bones and I will go."

"How are you going to go?" James says. "A half-dozen armed guards are blocking the exit."

The group looks at the guards scanning the crowd.

"Well how are *you* going to go then?" Reeko says.

James looks at the stocky guard near the podium.

"There's the service panel over there behind the podium," Philip says. "That leads directly into the lab where the Rover is."

"That passageway is too tight," Melissa says. "Someone would have to be pencil thin."

They all look at Bones.

He shrugs. "What?"

"He'll fit," Philip says.

Bones raises his eyebrows. "First, you want me to go outside and work, and now you want me to crawl through a tunnel to hide from military guys with guns while there are explosions rocking us down here?"

"But it's Chop," Reeko says.

Bones nods. "Okay. If I get over to him, how am I going to get back?"

"Here, take this." James hands him a walkie-talkie. "We'll wait for your call and figure something out."

Melissa exhales. "We need a distraction."

"I'll take care of that," James says, and then looks at Reeko. "Follow me."

"Be careful," Janice says, holding Brian tightly.

Brian looks at his dad with confidence in his eyes.

Bones sneaks through the crowd and over to the side of the podium. Two army guys stand guard near a metal grate on the wall. One has a snake tattoo on his neck. The other is baldheaded. And they share the same glare.

Alex and Brian watch James move toward a ventilation duct as Reeko follows.

"Your dad is pretty smart," Alex says.

Brian smiles. "He's going to save us."

James pulls out a flashlight and checks the fan above their heads.

The two army guys stare at him.

Bones snakes to the side near the grate.

"You smell that?" James says.

"Uh, yeah, I definitely do," Reeko replies.

The two army guys charge over.

Bones hustles as he pops the grate off, slips inside, and then re-attaches it.

"Hey, what are you two doing?" the army guy with the snake tattoo says.

James shines the light on the fan blades. "I'm a tech level four here and this is my colleague. We smell something strange. It might be the lubricant on the fan dripping onto the voltage regulator."

"I don't smell anything," the baldheaded army guy says.

"We should stop the fan and check the grease fitting," Reeko says.

The tattooed guy chews on the corner of his lip. "You two look familiar."

"Yeah," the baldheaded guy adds.

"Let's get that ladder over there and pull the plug," James says, gesturing.

The tattooed guy nods. "Hey. You're the two guys going to the surface to fix the shields."

"Yeah, where're your other crew members?" the baldheaded guard says.

Reeko goes to get the ladder.

"Oh, they're just in back there with family," James says, pointing at the crowd. "Can you guys help us hold the ladder?"

Through the grate, Bones crawls across the shaft. His bony body barely fits through the narrow space. Darkness surrounds him. The heat from above steals his sweat. The smell of sewage chokes him. He sees a light thirty yards away.

Back in the common area, James stands on a ladder assessing the blades. The smell of heat pours down.

"You're right, I smell something," the tattooed military guy says.

The baldheaded guy nods. "Smells like heat."

Reeko twitches his nose. "Yeah, it *is* heat."

James puts his hand up to the opening and feels the warmth.

Melissa comes over. "What did you do?" she whispers to Reeko.

"Nothing, ma'am. Honest."

James steps down. "That heat is coming down through the shields."

Melissa looks at the clock: "6:07."

James stares at the grate.

Down the corridor, Bones is five yards away from the end of the tunnel. Sweat covers his face and saturates his shirt.

He makes it to the end, the grate breaking up the light. There's silence on the other side. The open lab is still with the Rover parked halfway on the simulated rocks.

When Bones puts his hands on the grate, the sound of a male voice approaches, "This area needs to be checked next."

Bones freezes as the sound of silence returns.

He pops off the grate; it hits the floor, the noise filling the room. Bones slides inside, pressing his lips together as he reattaches it. He scurries to the Rover. "Chop? Are you there?" he whispers.

"Bones?" Chop replies, popping out from the back of the Rover. "How'd you get here?"

"Through the service shaft," Bones says, gesturing to the grate. "What the hell's going on, man?"

"I was in the supply room listening to some Led Zeppelin when the shaking started. I just thought it was you screwing around on the Rover so I kept loading my pack. After about ten minutes, I came out and everyone was gone. I went over to see if Mrs. Mercer was in her office, but I saw a full-bird colonel inside rooting around. So I stopped to see what he was doing, and I saw him planting what looked like C-4 under her desk."

Bones' eyes go wide. "What?"

"I know. I waited till he left, and then I went in there. It's C-4. I disarmed it," Chop says, handing Bones a ticking clock and wire.

"Whoa, I don't want that shit."

"It's disarmed."

"I don't care."

"Sir, this is the last area that needs to be checked," the male voice says.

Chop looks at the Rover, then the workbench, and then the silver UVASUITs. "Over here," he says to Bones.

Chop leads the way to the UVASUITs. He unlocks his and jumps inside, putting the disarmed bomb inside with him. Bones follows suit.

Two young military men amble in, each holding a smart tablet. The screens show meters ranging from 0 to 100 with "Explosive Detector" labeled at the top of the applications. On both, the numbers hover around "5."

"Is it hot in here or is it just me?" the taller one says.

"It's damn hot in here."

"Just hurry up, the colonel just wants us to sweep this area. He already got the offices," the taller one says.

Bones and Chop see the guards approaching. They look at each other through the face shields and widen their eyes.

The shorter soldier continues toward the Rover. The number on his smart tablet shows, "15." "What is this stuff anyway?"

"This is where they're training for the outside mission," the taller soldier says, assessing the workbench.

The shorter soldier goes to the suits. He looks inside one and sees Bones staring forward, sweat running down his nose. "Look how realistic these test dummies are. There's even sweat on them."

The taller soldier comes over and looks at Chop's frozen stare. "Look at this one. It has a handlebar mustache."

Both of their smart tablets show "85" on the scale.

"I think these are those new suits," the taller one says. "They're probably made of some synthetic material that's giving these sensors a fuckin' fit."

"Let's go," the shorter soldier says.

Both men leave the area.

The suits open and Bones and Chop step out.

"Shit, man," Bones says.

Chop wheezes. "We gotta get to Mrs. Mercer."

Bones pulls out the walkie-talkie and presses the side button. "James, you there?"

A hundred yards away, James and Reeko are checking a thermostat on the wall. James grabs the walkie-talkie. "James here."

"Yo, man. Big problems. Get Mercer over here."

"Negative. It's still hot over here," James says, staring at the military men.

"We've got bigger problems than just heat."

23

A painting of George Washington hangs on the wall. His slight smile is confident and his eyes are buoyant.

President Brooks wipes the sweat from his face and puts on his jacket. He fixes his lapel pin of an American flag. The president walks over to the painting and looks deep into Washington's eyes as he takes a deep breath filled with heat. "In God we trust," President Brooks whispers.

A knock sounds at the door. Ross peeks in. "Sir, we have thirty minutes left."

President Brooks exhales. He sits down at his desk as George Washington looks out behind him.

"Ross, I'd like to ask you a question," President Brooks says.

Ross walks in and closes the door behind him. "Yes, sir."

"How old are you, son?"

"I'm twenty-two."

"Twenty-two years old." The president chuckles. "Wow, a lot has changed since I was twenty-two." He exhales. "Ross, what do you think the world will be like when you reach my age?"

Ross takes a deep breath and looks at the painting of George Washington. "Sir, I don't think—"

Secretary Dunner barges into the office. "Queue up News One," he shouts at Ross. "President Brooks, quadrant one is gone."

The images on the screen show a vending cart burning, people lying in the open area, sprinklers showering the area with water.

Ross starts crying.

"I just told you to queue it up," Secretary Dunner says. "Now get out of here."

"Wait, what's wrong?" the president asks Ross.

"My aunt lives in quadrant one."

Secretary Dunner shrugs. "Casualties of war."

"That's enough," the president says. "I'm sorry, son. Go call your family."

"Thank you, sir." Ross leaves, shutting the door.

"More C-4 charges went off. This is beyond just those in the hospital."

"How many are dead?" the president asks.

"Easily hundreds, probably thousands. I lost a dozen of my men. They quarantined off quadrant one. No one in, no one out. There are terrorists out there."

"We're falling apart here," President Brooks says, swallowing hard.

"We've got to flush 'em out. I have my forces scanning the areas for the terrorists. There's something up at UVASHIELD."

"UVASHIELD? This whole plan doesn't work without their expertise."

"There's a damn mole there. I know it. I will find him, or should I say *her*."

"What did you do over there?"

"I had my guys do a full sweep of their spaces, looking for more explosives. You think I'm going to let some prissy in a business suit terrorize us and make demands?"

"Secretary Dunner, I trust your judgment with defending this nation. But you can't just shut things down without looking at the big picture. That's *my* job, remember?"

The president presses a button on his communication tablet. "Get Melissa Mercer on the video. Where are we with the lottery?"

A female voice responds, "Sir, the census folks are finalizing the list."

"Thank you," he says.

Secretary Dunner shakes his head. "This list is a joke. Come on. Why save these barbaric rats?"

"Cut the shit." President Brooks leans forward, fire in his eyes. "You're not the president. *I am*. These barbaric rats you're talking about are Americans. Last time I checked, we're all created equal."

Secretary Dunner looks at the painting of George Washington. "America is just a dream."

"I expect you to control these terrorists and support this effort that I am leading. Once I go live, I need you to facilitate getting those thousand on the list and bringing them to safety in the protected spaces inside quadrant two. Are we stockpiling everything of value there?"

"How should I know? I'm just worrying about defense," the secretary says, a scowl on his face.

A young woman in a business suit knocks on the door. "Sir, I have Mrs. Mercer from UVASHIELD on a video call."

"Put her on," he says.

The young woman enters and presses a few buttons. The image of Melissa pops up on a 32" flat-screen monitor. She's sitting in a conference room, her pale skin washing out on the screen.

"Melissa, can you hear me?" the president says.

"Yes, sir."

"How are things there?"

"We just got back to work. The military locked us down. There's something important that I must tell you. It's regarding Secretary Dunner."

Secretary Dunner looks at the president and puts his finger to his lips.

"Is he there with you, sir?" Melissa continues.

"Go ahead, Mrs. Mercer. We don't have much time."

"Sir, I think he's planning something. I don't know what. But he's trying to frame me and my company. He's, uh…"

"What are you trying to say, Mrs. Mercer?" the president says.

"I think he's a terrorist."

The president takes a deep breath and looks at Secretary Dunner.

The secretary's eyes widen, which deepens the wrinkles in his brow. "I'm not going to sit here and listen to this bitch! How dare you call me a terrorist! *You're* the terrorist. I'll prove it." Secretary Dunner clicks his smart tablet. "Colonel Drake, are you still at UVASHIELD?"

"Uh, roger that, sir."

"Have your men search Melissa Mercer's office right now."

On the video, Melissa moves to the door, but the tattooed military guy busts it open. She screams. He grabs her arm, while the two young soldiers come in and scan the room with their smart tablets.

Melissa jerks her arm, but the military guy strengthens his grip. She concedes and simply stands, surrounded by the stench of the guy's sweat.

The president crosses his arms as the secretary sits back and laces his fingers.

The colonel comes in and oversees his men.

"Clear, sir," both young soldiers say.

The secretary says into his smart tablet, "Colonel, have them check everywhere. Visually inspect under her desk."

"Roger."

One of the young soldiers bends down and crawls under the desk. It shakes from his movement, which knocks the picture of the Mercer family onto the ground.

Glass shatters, a piece piercing her heart.

The secretary cracks his knuckles.

The young soldier stands up. "It's all clear, sir."

The president sits up. "Let her go. This is ridiculous."

The secretary shakes his head. "Colonel." He bites his lip.

"Yes, sir."

"Tell your men to stand down," the secretary says. "Let her go."

The colonel exhales. "Let's go, men."

The tattooed military guy releases Melissa, who glares at him. He smirks as he leaves with everyone. She sits back down.

The president's face is red. He slams his fist down on the table. "Listen, everyone. I'm the president. Enough of these games. Everyone just do their job." He sits back. "Now, Mrs. Mercer. Tell me about your team. Are they ready to go live in twenty minutes?"

"Yes, sir. My team is ready. The suits are reinforced."

"Now, Secretary Dunner. Your job is to facilitate the safe extraction of the individuals selected by the lottery, and to oversee the security of our citizens."

The secretary sits back.

"Am I clear?!" the president shouts.

"Yes... Sir..." the secretary says.

"Good. Now go do your jobs. I have a speech to prepare."

Secretary Dunner leaves.

The president presses a button, killing the image on the screen. He picks up the phone. "Ross, come here."

The president stands up and looks at the wrinkles on the face of George Washington.

24

The photograph of the Mercer family lies on the ground. Melissa reaches for it, but a piece of broken glass slices her finger. She shrieks as blood forms in the wound.

She sits up. The lights dim in the room. Melissa blinks rapidly, keeping her mind in reality.

She wraps her finger with a tissue. Inside the top drawer, she removes a prescription bottle of liquid and swallows a mouthful.

The clock on the wall reads, "6:42."

Melissa sits back and takes a deep breath. The heat in the air chokes her. She stands up, leaves the office, and then moves toward the lab.

Inside, a scientist checks his smart tablet. The racks holding the suits are empty.

"Mrs. Mercer," Philip says, walking into the lab. "How did the meeting go with the president?"

An army guy walks by in the distance.

"Don't ask," she says. "Are the guys suited up?"

"Yes, ma'am. They are in the landing area with the television crew."

"Television crew?"

"Yes, the president's office sent them. They are going to broadcast their departure before the president's speech."

Blood saturates the tissue.

"Mrs. Mercer, you're bleeding."

"I'll be fine," she says, wrapping more tissues around the wound. "Let's go."

Melissa and Philip move down the corridor.

"Is everyone safe?" Melissa asks.

"Everyone is back where they came from. But the heat. People are asking about the heat."

They walk past a young military woman.

"Is Lance still around?" Melissa whispers to Philip.

"Yes, and he said he is standing by."

Through another corridor, they move toward a large bay door that says, "Landing Deck – UVASHIELD."

"Keep an eye on that one," the tattooed military guy says as Melissa approaches the guards at the entryway.

"What's going on, Mrs. Mercer?" Philip asks.

"Let's keep moving," she replies.

Both show their badges. The guards let them through the checkpoint.

The area is like the deck of a battleship. Camouflaged helicopters are parked in bays, dwarfing the smaller transport choppers. Two dozen military personnel stand guard. A TV crew works cameras and lighting equipment. In the middle of it all, some scientists check the Rover, while others assess Reeko, Bones, and Chop.

Melissa steps toward the group. "Those suits okay?" she asks a couple of scientists checking the four suits.

"They will hold up," the scientist with the thick glasses replies.

She moves to Chop, Bones, and Reeko. "Where's James?"

"Still with his family," Reeko says.

"He needs to be down here," Melissa says, and then looks at Philip. "Go fetch him, please."

"Any updates?" Chop whispers to Melissa as they both eye the military members clutching their weapons.

She shakes her head. "You guys just worry about up there. I'll worry about down here."

"Are you okay, ma'am?" Reeko says, looking at her bloody tissue.

"I'll be fine."

A woman wearing a business suit approaches. "Mrs. Mercer, we just arrived. We're with News One. Will you be speaking?"

"Who sent you?"

"The president's office."

A portly guy holding a video camera comes over. His eyes have a look of despair. "Hey, can you hook me up with a lottery pass?"

"Why are you here?" Melissa says. "You must leave or I'm going to call security."

"They stay," the colonel says. He looks at the TV woman in the suit. "Mercer should say a few words while you show the crew on camera. And make her up. She looks like shit." The colonel sees the scientists checking the crew. "Where's the fourth one anyway?"

Through the dense walls and into the bank of suites, the lights are off inside one of the rooms, and it's warm inside, like the warmth offered by the sun on a summer afternoon at a beach in Virginia. Yet humidity laces the air and makes it smell as if it's from a beach further south, a beach in Florida. While darkness surrounds the room and the sound of stillness prevails, there exists the sound of a beat. At further inspection, the sound reveals itself as three distinct beats, one beating eighty times per minute, the second beating ninety times per minute, and the third beating one hundred and twenty times per minute.

"Your heart's racing," Janice whispers.

"Are you okay, Dad?" Brian asks.

James grips his family nestled in his arms, lying on two cots pushed together. He responds by squeezing them slightly, enough for them to know that he's there.

Silence returns as their ears go back to the beating hearts. James slows his breathing, timing it with his wife's and with his son's. As time moves forward, their breathing converges as one, but their hearts still beat off-key, and there's not enough time for them to join each other.

"Three to two," James whispers.

"What?" Janice says.

"The score was three to two. I couldn't block the last shot, for the championship."

"The game?" Janice says.

"We were ahead the whole game, and then they tied it with two minutes to go. We were still tied when there were ten seconds left. They shot the ball. It was right there in front of me. Right there. I can still see it. I went for it, but it just slipped through my hands at the goal."

"Don't live this out in your mind for the rest of your life," Janice says.

"Then the Earth started shaking. I just laid there on the ground. I saw my dad, my mom. She was crying. I could've helped them, if I just ran to them. I know I could've helped them."

"Dad," Brian says.

"Yeah, tiger."

"Are you going on a suicide mission?"

"Brian, stop," Janice says.

"No, it's okay. Son, I may not be able to come back."

Janice squeezes his arm. "James, you stop it, now."

"Why hide from it, right? Who knows if these suits will last? Who knows what's up there? I should just stay here. With both of you. This would be a nice way to spend the rest of our time together, don't you think?"

A quiver of fear flows through the cots. Brian is crying.

"Why are you giving up?" Janice asks.

"Who says I'm giving up? We have choices in life and I choose to stay here with you."

"You're a coward," she says.

James remains silent. He grips his son as he loses the grip on his wife. "What do you want me to do?" he says. "Go out there and get killed?"

Janice flips on the light switch. The lights stab their eyes.

"I want you to go out there and do your job. Provide for your family."

"Ah, come on." He sits up. "Just say that you want me to go on a suicide mission. Go ahead."

"You gotta be kidding," Janice says, laughing.

Someone knocks on the door.

"Who is it?" Janice asks, staring at the closed door.

"Uh, it's Philip. Where is Mr. Wilson?"

"He's in here."

"It's time, sir."

"Give us a minute," James shouts.

"What do you want to do?" Janice says.

James holds his breath and stares at a crack in the floor.

Janice looks at the pink fabric on the bathrobe in the closet.

Brian stops crying. He walks to his bag in the corner and removes the item that he found in the trash, the item that he hid under his bed in his room, the item that he wanted to give to his father as a birthday gift. Brian places the item on the cot.

Memories flow through James' mind—kicking a soccer ball with his dad in the backyard, kicking it around cones during school practice, kicking it before the championship game, before the chaos.

"Where'd you get that?" James asks, looking at the deflated soccer ball.

"I found it. After work today, can you teach me how to play soccer, Dad?"

James breaks down. Tears flow from his eyes.

Janice sits down next to him, tears rolling down her cheeks.

Brian stands over his parents and puts his arms around them.

"Don't be afraid, Dad," Brian whispers.

"I'm sorry," James says. "I'm so sorry."

"It's my fault," Janice says. "I shouldn't have pressured you all this time. It's your decision."

James stands up. "I will teach you how to play soccer, son, but you have to promise me one thing."

"What, Dad?"

"You have to get this ball inflated before I get home from work."

"I promise, Dad," Brian says, hugging him.

Janice stands up and hugs her husband and her son.

Philip knocks again. "Mr. Wilson."

James wipes his tears and opens the door. "I'm ready."

25

A seven-year-old boy holding a RoboDog kneels in an alcove. Heat rises from a grate. Murky water sprays from a pipe. Cockroaches fornicate in a puddle. The boy blinks his eyes and licks his cracked lips.

A woman runs past through the corridor as two soldiers hustle after her. Her screams find their way back to the boy and provoke tears in his eyes.

The dog barks.

"Shh, it'll be okay," the boy whispers, petting the dog.

It wags its tail and nestles up against his dirty T-shirt.

"Hey!" an angry voice shouts.

The boy sees a tall soldier peering down at him. He clutches the dog and scurries further into the alcove.

"What are you doing back here?" The tall soldier squeezes in, grabs the boy's shirt, and then pulls him out. "You can't be out here. Where're your parents?"

"I lost my mom," the boy says, crying.

The tall soldier picks the boy up and moves down the corridor. More military men approach. The boy closes his eyes and clutches his dog.

"Matthew!" a woman shouts.

The boy looks at the woman, his mother, held by another guard. Both mother and son run to each other and embrace.

The tall military man smiles. His breathing slows, and his eyes narrow.

"They can't be here," the short soldier says. "Send them to the slush pile."

"Where did you guys come from?" the tall soldier asks the boy and the mother.

"We got separated in the common area," the mother says. "My sister is somewhere there."

"Just put them in with the others. We have to clear this area," the short soldier says to his comrade.

The tall soldier takes a deep breath filled with heat and sewage. "Come on. Hurry. There's a shortcut."

The short soldier shakes his head.

"Thank you," the mother says. She looks at her son. "Hurry."

The tall soldier leads them down a corridor. He cuts through an abandoned store with damaged metal racks and with clothes on the ground.

"Watch the glass," the tall soldier says.

They exit out the back and move down another corridor. At a doorway, four guards stand with their rifles.

The mother holds her son tightly.

"These two belong in here," the tall soldier says.

"Come on, man," the guard with the goatee says. "The stragglers need to be put in area B. Not here."

"They're missing family."

The guards relinquish their stance.

Through the doorway, hundreds of people stand in the common area. Some people shout. Some people cry. Some people sleep. Some people die.

Suddenly, a dozen people push to come back through the doorway. The guards go in and shove the individuals back.

The tall soldier brings the mother and son in to join the crowd.

"Thank you. Thank you," the mother says, scurrying inside with her son.

The tall soldier sees another woman run up to them. They all hug. He blinks slowly, watching with compassion.

"What time is it?" one of the soldiers asks.

"Seven o'clock," another one replies.

The twenty-foot screen flickers. The image of the president displays. The wrinkles in his forehead are deeper. His skin is pale.

The people quiet down. Others wake up. A few people boo.

"My fellow Americans. It is seven o'clock in the morning on July nineteenth, twenty forty-five. It is time for us to write another chapter in American history. Like you, I wish this whole thing were a dream. I wish that everything were a mistake. But we're not dreaming. We are awake at this hour to confront this problem. Our first order of business should be met with optimism. Leaders in government and industry have been working tirelessly around the clock to facilitate the reinforcement of the shield systems on the surface. Mrs. Melissa Mercer of UVASHIELD has led this effort."

Several boos fill the area.

"Mrs. Mercer has sacrificed herself, her family, and her company to make this happen. *Her team* is now *our team*. We are ready to watch them, to support them, to pray for them."

The image switches to the landing deck of UVASHIELD. Melissa addresses the camera in the center frame as Philip stands to her side. Behind her are James, Chop, Bones, and Reeko. Richard, Alex, Janice, and Brian stand in front of a crowd of scientists and military personnel. The Rover and its trailer, as well as the four silver suits, are on the side of the crowd.

"Thank you," Melissa says. The camera tightens on her slightly. Her face is pale and her eyes are sad. "Donald Trump, the successful business owner, once said, 'You have to think anyway, so why not think big?' Well, my business, my passion, is now able to provide the ultimate service, the service to you, to all of humanity. This day is not about me; it's about the team right behind me. These individuals have worked nonstop since this news broke only forty-eight hours ago. Their families are here to support them in this endeavor. My husband, Richard, and my son, Alex, are here with me as well."

Melissa nods at her husband and son and gives them a sad smile.

Richard kisses his palm and sends her the kiss.

"I would like to say thank you for your support in life," Melissa says. "And now, I would like to give each member of our ground team a moment to say a word."

The four guys step forward and stand next to Melissa.

"Go ahead," she says.

Reeko grins. "Uh, I want to say 'I love you' to my mom and dad. They're looking down on me from above. I'll do my best up there."

Bones looks into the camera and nods. "All I want to say is that when we get back, the first round is definitely *not* on me."

Chop twirls his mustache. "I'm doing this for all the ladies out there, real and simulated. Remember my name, *Chop!*"

The camera goes to James, who stares blankly.

The crowd in the common area watches him.

"Come on, brother," Chop whispers. "Say something from the heart."

James smiles. "I'm doing this for my family, and for your family. I'm not afraid to go up there because my wife and my son are always with me." He looks at them with heavy eyes.

Chop leans over to the mic. "Before we leave, before the president announces who's staying and who's not, I think we owe it to ourselves to take a moment to be together, to celebrate the history of America and for all the great people out there. And I want to dedicate this moment to my coworker, my best friend, James Wilson." Chop hugs James. Janice looks on and smiles.

"And you know," Chop continues. "This guy is in love with that woman over there—his wife of twelve years. You know, Janice, he always turns us down for a drink after work to be with you and Brian. And you know, James told me that he never had his first dance with you after your wedding. He said you guys couldn't afford a big wedding because we know that the wages back then were shit."

"They're still shit!" Bones says.

Chop looks at Melissa and smiles. "Sorry, kids. Don't repeat that. So, James, I feel that while we are all here now, while everyone is bonded together, let's pause and listen to the best singer who ever lived." Chop nods at a geeky guy standing by the news chopper.

The beat of the drums expels from two speakers next to the geeky guy. Everyone freezes.

"This is for you, brother," Chop says as he steps aside and joins everyone.

The smooth-as-glass voice of Al Green fills the space with "Let's Stay Together."

James' cheeks flush. Janice smiles and covers her eyes.

The sound pumps into the common areas of the remaining quadrants.

Workers in quadrant two watch James on the big screen. Men and women in quadrant six stop fighting and stare at the same images on the screen. The boy, his mother, and his aunt watch James from inside the crowd in quadrant four. The president, Ross, and a dozen staff members observe the same images from the conference room.

James holds his breath, feeling the eyes of tens of thousands of people on him. His heart races. His pores sweat. His lungs cry for air. Should he run? Should he hide? His senses panic. As his mind races with thoughts of people laughing, he simply raises his hand.

As if love were a magnet, Janice gravitates toward her husband.

Al Green's voice goes high as the soft beat of the drums consumes the entire underground space and flows through the population of America.

Janice accepts James' hand and she lets him scoop her up. He guides her waist, left and then right, to the beat of the drums. James exhales, the moisture in his breath tickling the soft skin of his wife's neck. She rests her head under his chin and feels his warmth against her cheek. James inhales a deep breath of his wife, his life, his love. They dance as one, slowly, happily. They dance as if the world is theirs, and for this moment in time, it is.

Melissa steps over to Richard and Alex. She falls into her husband's arms.

Brian watches his mother and father smiling. Tears form in his eyes, tears of love, tears of happiness.

The people in the common areas watch the couple dance. The mother, son, and aunt hold each other. No one fights. No one pillages. No one raises a gun. No one shouts. That's because everyone has become one.

As Al Green's voice fades, James grips his wife and twirls her. She lets out a giggle, a sound that goes through his ears and into his mind, bypassing memories of darkness, tragedy, and death, retrieving an image of his wedding night with this woman.

Silence ensues. Then a wave of clapping and cheering erupts, which flows through the quadrant walls.

Janice looks deep into her husband's eyes and grips his soul. She kisses him.

A wave of energy surges from the crowd.

"I love you," he whispers.

"I love you, my husband," she says. "Don't be afraid."

They turn to face their audience; it's their wedding day again.

Reeko gives them the thumbs up. Bones is clapping, but then he uses the distraction to sneak a gulp from a flask. Chop runs over with Brian in his arms. James picks up Brian as mother, father, and son embrace.

Chop uses his hands to present the couple. The clapping intensifies again.

"Thank you," James says to Chop.

"You guys are beautiful."

"I love you, Dad," Brian says, still in his arms.

James smiles and hugs them again. "I love you both with my whole heart."

Janice looks at Chop. "Bring him home safely."

"He's coming home in style," Chop says.

The crowd simmers down as the camera goes back to Melissa. She's crying.

James, Chop, Bones, and Reeko go to the Rover. A dozen scientists jump to action and open up the silver suits for them. Each man steps inside, and then the scientists seal the suits.

"Just like in training," the young female scientist says to Bones.

They sit down in the Rover as the scientists secure their packs. The platform to the world above lowers down from the ceiling.

A gray-haired scientist attaches four small pouches to the rear compartment of the Rover. "Special fire extinguishers. Open only in case of emergency."

Bones starts the engine. It rumbles boldly.

James looks at Janice and Brian and gives them a thumps up. Janice sends him a kiss as Brian waves.

The Rover drives onto the platform. Two red lights flash as the platform ascends toward the opening in the ceiling.

The mother, aunt, and son watch the platform rise on the big screen.

"Where are they going, Mom?" the boy asks.

"To the surface to save us," his mom replies.

Once the platform ascends beyond the view, a cold breeze cuts through the heat and flows through every person's body in the underground.

The president cuts back onto the screen. His eyes are moist. He licks his lips and clears his throat. "I wish we could end it at that. I wish those four brave men were going to fix a shield that could sustain all of us down here. But we must take care of the business in front of us. The process to select one thousand individuals has been completed. There was no magic formula based on age, gender, marital status, or income. The only way to do this was with random numbers. What about families who will be broken, loved ones who could be left behind? What if you refuse to go? Although I wish we had enough time to look at each individual situation, well, we simply *don't* have enough time. There is only *one* rule. You may give your ticket away, but this must be on your own free will. With that said, I ask that you do not resort to violence. Please, as Americans, this can only work if you make it work. There will be increased military personnel ensuring the civility and safety of this process."

The military in the common area of quadrant four stand guard with riot gear.

The president continues, "The ticket is your key, and your key will allow entry into the special area in quadrant two. The clock is ticking, and it is ticking faster than we could estimate." On the screen, a clock superimposes: "0 days, 11 hours, 51 minutes, 49 seconds."

"They changed it," Richard says. "There are less than twelve hours remaining."

"Even that number could change," Melissa replies, wiping the sweat from under her eyes.

The president says, "Once you are issued your key, you will have less than twelve hours before the gates close. Tonight at seven o'clock. You may ask about those who did not get a ticket. Well, we are not abandoning you. We will provide every available resource, child care, medical care, support groups, to allow life to live as long as possible. We are already experiencing the increased heat. Temperatures have risen from eighty degrees in the common areas to ninety; some places are already near one hundred." The president exhales. "So the time has come. The list will be available on every smart connected device throughout our underground nation. From your personal device to the jumbo smart screens in the common areas, the numbers will be displayed. To claim your ticket, there will be stations set up in each common area verifying those selected by biometric fingerprints. If you are selected and do not wish to give away your ticket, it is advisable to conceal this ticket and proceed directly to the gates in quadrant two. These gates will be open in two hours." The president narrows his eyes at the camera. "I wish you luck. America loves each and every one of you. In God we trust."

The image goes to black on the screen. In quadrant four, shouts come from the crowd: "It's all a lie!" and "We're dead!"

The military personnel stand guard. A helicopter lowers down into a side area that troops are guarding. Five army men rappel from the chopper and join the other soldiers.

The boy looks up at his mom and aunt. "Why are there so many army people?"

"For our safety, baby," his mom says.

The chopper lands. A man in shorts runs toward the chopper and hurls a stone. Three soldiers pounce on him and pull him back.

A man with glasses steps out from the chopper. He's holding a smart tablet and a card printer.

Suddenly on the screens, a list of one thousand numbers pops up.

The mother sees an abandoned restaurant with a dozen ten-inch tablets at each table showing the same list.

"Over here," she says, pulling her sister and son.

A mob storms the same building. The mother clutches her son as the crowd pushes her sister away. The boy drops his RoboDog and a burly man smashes it.

"Sis!" the mother shouts.

A crazy man with a gun fires into the crowd. People shriek.

The mother shields her son as the crazy man fires more shots. A bullet hits an elderly man, sending him down hard. People trample him.

Four military men fire toward the crazy man.

"Mom! Help Auntie!" the boy screams.

The mother sees her sister, but then time stops. A bullet from the crazy man's gun hits her sister in the chest and tears through her heart.

The boy locks eyes with his aunt, and then life escapes through her eyes.

"No!" the mother shouts.

The military men pump the crazy man's chest with bullets, sending his body to the ground.

One of the military men grabs the weapon. "Secure!"

A man and a woman in work suits toss the crazy man's body onto a cart. Then they move toward the mother's sister.

"No! Mom! Help her!"

The mother starts crying. They toss her sister's body onto the pile and cart her away.

"Area sanitized," another military man says into a walkie-talkie.

The mother and her son roll into the building. She grabs a smart tablet on the floor as the crowd flutters around. She scrolls through the list using her finger, and then she sets down the tablet. Tears pour from her eyes.

"Did we make the list, Mom?"

She squeezes her son tightly, the answer to the question in her tears.

26

A sign reads, "Warning! UVASUIT required to proceed further. Two-man check required."

The platform stops.

James stands up from his spot in the Rover. "Can you guys hear me?"

"Loud and clear," Reeko replies.

"Roger," Bones says.

"Like a cat in a crib," Chop goes.

James shakes his head and exhales. "So who wants to do the honors?"

Reeko steps out and walks to the other side of the platform lift where a button is flashing red.

"Everyone's suit okay?" Reeko says.

James looks at his heads-up display in the corner of his field of vision. It reads, "Oxygen Level: 99%, Internal Temperature: 73, External Temperature: 109."

"Roger," they all say together.

"This is it, ladies. These damn suits better work." Reeko puts his finger on the button. He looks at James, whose finger is resting on a similar button. "On three."

James nods. "One...two...*three.*"

They both press their buttons at the same time. A buzzer sounds, and then the cart ascends. James and Reeko go back to their seats.

"Guys, this is control. Can you hear me? Over."

"They're in my head," Chop says.

"Copy, control. We can hear you," James says.

"Once you're up there and off the platform, you're on your own. Signals are worthless on the surface."

"Roger that," James says.

"You guys should have thirteen hours of air in those suits. Stick to the course and you should be back in twelve."

"Trust us, we're going to get this shit done fast," Bones says, gripping the wheel.

"Okay, guys. Good luck. We...you...best," the voice says, breaking up.

A bay door opens above their heads. The platform goes up into a cave and stops. A chain-link doorway opens. Rock surrounds them, only the light from the Rover shining.

"Where exactly are we?" Bones asks.

A sign next to James reads, "Return access to underground requires person to be wearing UVASUIT – Press Button from inside UVASUIT for re-entry."

"Well, we need to be wearing one of these to get back," James says. "Must be a chip in them."

"Trust me, I'm not taking this thing off," Chop says, seeing "External Temperature: 130" in his heads-up display.

As the suits adjust to the limited light, a passageway appears ahead.

"Hold on!" Bones puts the Rover into gear and drives it off the platform onto the gravelly terrain.

The walls are thick with stones jutting at every angle.

Bones moves the Rover five miles an hour through the surrounding darkness. Suddenly, the headlights reflect off something near the wall.

"Wait. Over there," Chop says, gesturing toward the reflection.

The Rover slows down and approaches the wall of the cave. Chop presses a button on the forearm of his suit. Two lights shine forward on his helmet.

He gets out of the Rover and sees something buried in the gravel.

It's a Pennsylvania license plate.

Chop grabs it and places it on the back of the trailer attached to the Rover. "Now, we're legal."

"Let's go," Reeko says.

Chop jumps back inside.

Bones drives the Rover faster as the guys watch the headlights shine onto rocks.

"This reminds me of the haunted house at Disney World," Chop says.

"Bones, speed it up," Reeko says.

The Rover accelerates. A sharp right turn is up ahead. Bones slows down and makes the turn. They pass a metal fan blade half-buried in the sand.

Fifty yards of cave lead to a spot of light. The Rover races toward it, the light growing in size.

James takes a deep breath as they near the light, and then their eyes catch fire. A wall of orange surrounds them. Their suits try to compensate, their helmets adjusting the shade.

Bones disorients. He squeezes the throttle.

The guys bounce and jostle.

"Brakes! Brakes!" Reeko shouts.

"My eyes!" Chop says.

James holds on, the fire trying to seep past his eyelids.

A bounce rocks their bodies and sends their packs off the side.

The Rover finally stops.

The heavily filtered light reaches James' eyes. A rocky hill is above them. Rocks and dust surround the area. The sky is orange.

"Is everyone okay?" James says.

"I can see now," Chop replies.

"I'm okay," Bones says.

Reeko flails his arms. "No! No! It's too bright!"

James bangs on Reeko's helmet.

The helmet beeps and filtered light reaches Reeko's eyes. "Shit, man. My eyes are burning."

"Somebody should've broken in these suits," Bones says.

Chop looks at the external temperature sensor on his heads-up display. "One hundred ninety."

"Damn. How does everyone feel?" Reeko says.

Chop taps his chest. "Like a sardine."

James sees two packs on the ground so he jumps out and grabs them.

"What are in those emergency pouches they gave us?" Bones asks.

"I don't think this counts as an emergency," James says.

James and Reeko secure the packs to the Rover.

"How will we know how to get back here?" Chop asks.

Bones points at a screen on the Rover showing three points. "This is where we are, this is the bridge, and this is the first shield. We have about fifty miles to travel."

"Let's go," Reeko says.

Bones puts the Rover into gear and moves over some rocks toward a large field of gravel. Skyscrapers stand tall in the distance. A burned-out truck sits ten yards away.

"Is that AMG?" Chop goes.

"What?" Reeko says.

"Yeah, it is. I used to work for that company back in the tens."

"Enough with the memories," Reeko says. "I just want to get done with this job and get home."

"Home?" Bones says. "We may not have a home to go back to."

James sees a metal placard hiding under a rock. There are three stick figures on it with the words *Family Restroom*.

27

A man stands on the side of the Ben Franklin Bridge ready to jump. A car races toward him, but before it can reach the man, he falls over the side.

"What are you boys doing?" Janice asks, sitting at the table with Richard and sharing simulated coffee.

"Nothing," Alex and Brian say at the same time, playing with the man and the car on their model.

"Do you think your dad is there yet?" Alex asks Brian.

"No. I think it takes a while."

Alex growls while bopping one of the figures around the bridge. "Do you think he'll find any monsters up there?"

Brian moves the car across the bridge. "I think he'll find all the answers."

Melissa opens the door and comes in; her face is as gray as a stillborn baby.

"Mom," Alex says. "Do you think Brian's dad will find any monsters up there?"

"No, baby."

"Honey, you look horrible," Richard says.

"Nice to see you too," she replies.

"Sit down, Melissa," Janice says. "Have some s-coffee."

She sits down. "Thank you, but I need my medicine."

Richard grabs a glass from the cupboard and measures some yellow liquid from the prescription bottle.

"Are you okay?" Janice asks.

"I'm fine. There was a problem with the download to our area. The heat is slowing the bandwidth."

"The heat is slowing *me* down," Janice replies, wiping her neck.

"They should have the list to us soon."

Richard gives her the glass with the yellow liquid. "Did you hear from the doctor?"

"No. I've been too busy."

"Doctor? What's wrong?" Janice asks.

"She fell down and threw up," Alex says.

"Oh dear, I hope everything is alright."

The list displays on the smart tablet on the table and on the smart screen on the wall.

"Mom, the list is here," Brian says, running with Alex to the screen on the wall.

Melissa, Richard, and Janice look at the tablet.

Janice scrolls through the list. "Wait. Is this the complete list?"

"All one thousand," Richard says, pointing at the header.

Janice's eyes widen. "Brian, James, and I are not on here. There must be some mistake."

Richard fixes his glasses and scrolls through the list again. He squints his eyes.

"They're not there?" Melissa checks the list.

"I thought we had a deal, Mrs. Mercer," Janice says. "My husband was going to do this only in exchange for us being saved."

"What's that mean, Mom?" Brian says, moving next to her side. Alex goes to his father.

"This is wrong. I'm sure of it." Melissa storms out of the door.

In the hallway, a man comes out of his suite. A woman from another room joins him.

"Mrs. Mercer, we're not on the list," the man says.

"You lied!" the woman shouts.

"Just go back inside. I'm going to get to the bottom of this." She marches down the corridor and sees Philip in the distance. "Philip!"

"Mrs. Mercer, there you are," he says, rushing toward her.

"We just saw the list. Is there a problem with the transmission because of the heat?"

"No, ma'am," Philip says.

Two military men cheer in the distance.

"What's going on?" she asks Philip.

Three guys dance in front of the common area entryway.

Melissa digs her nails into her palms. "Come with me." She continues past the celebrating guys, their cheers stabbing her senses.

"Mrs. Mercer, something's wrong," a woman in a suit says from the side.

"Sit tight," Melissa replies. "We're working it."

She uses her fingerprint to enter her office door. Philip follows her.

"Get the president's office," she says.

Philip presses some buttons on the wall. The screen lights up with the UVASHIELD logo. Then the image changes to "Dialing… Office of the President."

Melissa takes a napkin and wipes the back of her neck.

The screen shows, "All circuits are busy."

"What?" Melissa says. "Keep trying." She goes to her desk, opens up her phone, and then presses a button to speed-dial the president's office.

A fast busy signal replies.

She slams her hand down on the desk. Philip jumps back. The bandage on her finger saturates with blood.

Melissa dials the secretary of defense's office. It rings on speakerphone.

"Secretary of Defense Dunner's office," a chipper female voice says.

"I need to speak with Secretary Dunner."

"Who is calling?"

"This is…uh," she starts to say, looking at Philip. "This is his helicopter pilot. We have a problem with his chopper."

"Oh, one moment, please."

Melissa shakes her head as she sees the "All circuits are busy" message still on the screen.

Philip steps closer to her.

"This is Dunner," his voice snakes through the speaker.

"What the hell is going on?" Melissa says.

"Who is this?" he replies.

"You know who this is, you little snake."

"Ahh, well, hey. Life is a business, right? You should know that."

"So what are you getting in return for selling your soul to the devil?"

"Hey, I didn't sell my soul to the devil. Those thousand people sold their souls to me. You should've kept on my good side."

"Cut the shit. We all had a deal."

"*Fuck you*, Mercer. I hope you burn down here with the rest of the rats."

She grinds her teeth. "The president is going to have your head."

"Uh, well, he's a bit *tied up* right now."

Through the phone and into his office, Secretary Dunner has his feet up on his desk. A painting of Aaron Burr hangs above him. Across the room is President Brooks, inside a cage, arms tied together, mouth gagged. He wriggles around inside.

"What did you do to the president?" Melissa says.

"The president? You're already talking to him," Secretary Dunner says, laughing. "Too bad those fine chaps up top are left in the dark, or should I say left in the light. Goodbye, Mrs. Mercer. I suggest you go be with your family. You only have ten hours left before you're sealed into your tomb."

The phone clicks.

Melissa throws the phone at the wall, smashing it into pieces.

Philip flinches. The hairs on the back of his neck stand up. He stares at the picture of Melissa holding baby Alex, nestled next to her husband. She's smiling, the warmth of her skin radiating, her eyes warm. However, the woman in front of him is grinding her teeth, her skin pale, her eyes cold.

"Is Lance here?" she says.

"Yes, ma'am." Philip swallows hard. "What are you going to do?"

Melissa stares into his eyes and clenches her fist.

28

A burned UVASUIT lies on the ground. Its helmet is cracked. James, Chop, Bones, and Reeko stand around the suit.

"Where's the body?" Chop asks.

"The fire got her," Reeko says.

Bones swallows. "I wonder what spooked her."

James sees the tractor-trailer ten yards away. He walks over to it, a reflection catching his eye.

"I think it was an accident," Chop says.

Bones shakes his head. "No. They said she saw something out here. A person."

Something sways under the tractor-trailer as James approaches.

"James!" Reeko shouts. "What the hell are you doing?"

James turns around and hurries back. "I thought I saw something moving."

"How about *we* keep moving?" Reeko says.

They walk back to the Rover. "I'm hungry," Chop says.

Bones gestures to a burned-out building; a faint outline of an "M" is still visible on its side. "There's a McDonald's. Why don't you go in and get me a Filet-O-Fish and a large fry."

Reeko smiles. "I'll take a Big Mac, large fry, and a chocolate shake."

"Get James a Happy Meal," Bones says.

They all chuckle.

"Who's paying?" Chop asks.

"It's on me this time," James says.

They sit back down in the Rover.

"What do we got in this suit anyway?" Chop says.

James uses his eyes to scroll through the heads-up display. A list of meals pops up. "Looks like simulated chicken with snow peas or simulated steak with mashed potatoes."

"No Filet-O-Fish?" Bones says.

"Come on, ladies," Reeko goes. "Stop dreaming. Let's eat and drive."

Chop, James, and Bones select the chicken and Reeko selects the steak. A straw drops down inside the suits. Each man sucks up his liquid. Bones pulls the Rover out as they drive through the gravelly downtown streets.

Chop nods. "Not bad."

"Don't get it on your mustache," Bones says.

James sees the outline of a bell in the distance. "Hey. Stop. There's the Liberty Bell."

Bones slows the Rover to a stop.

"Come on," Reeko says. "What is this? A trolley tour?"

"My son would love to see this. He did a presentation on this last month."

"Let's go," Reeko says, tapping Bones on the shoulder.

The Rover accelerates. They travel through the streets, navigating around burned-out cars, boulders, and sand piles. Around a turn, they arrive at a hole in the Earth. Bones hits the brake, stopping the Rover.

Chop peers over the side. "Unless this thing can fly, we have to find another way."

"Philly is a grid. We can just go down there to get around," James says, gesturing toward an adjacent street.

"We've got to move faster," Reeko says.

The Rover accelerates and zips along at forty miles an hour. Down another street, rocks block the way.

"Hold on!" Bones says.

They hit the rocks, bouncing over them. Chop gets some of his chicken in his moustache so he uses his tongue to clean it.

The ride smooths out and Bones speeds up. A skyscraper has become rubble on a city block. The shell of a military tank rests halfway through a concrete building.

On his heads-up display, James sees the outside temperature reading "211." The internal temperature shows, "79." He scrolls over to the word *Hydration* and selects it. Another straw lowers; he takes a long drink.

They pass a one-floor brick building extending for two blocks. Out front are two poles separated by about 30 yards. One pole has a half arch of a basketball backboard.

"All these people," James whispers.

"What's that?" Reeko says.

"All these people who used to call this their community, call this their home. It's been what, over ten years since I've been up here. And the remnants of these people are still here. Just think of all the people who didn't get the ticket to go underground. They died up here. And now we're faced with the same challenge, but now we're reducing ourselves to a thousand. What's next?"

"Zero," Bones says.

Chop stares at the horizon. "Where are they all?"

Bones shakes his head. "Dead."

"No. I mean, where are all the bodies? There were millions and millions of people. How did they just vanish?"

"Ashes to ashes," Bones says.

James scoops up a handful of sand from a pile collected near his feet. He lets it fall through his fingers. "And dust to dust."

"I remember driving through here back in the twenty-tens," Reeko says. "I had a two-thousand-two Cadillac Eldorado. Some twenty-inch wheels, lowered two inches. That was the ride."

"I was thirteen when we went underground," Bones says. "On the surface, I just remember going to school and hating it. My parents fought a lot and I stayed a lot at my grandmothers. She used to take me to the park."

"Did anyone in your family make it?" Reeko asks.

"Nah. I'm it. The last of the Bones."

Reeko nods slowly. "I hope they rest in peace, man."

"How about you, Chop?" Bones says.

"I was here like a week before going underground. I grew up in California, you guys know that."

"Tell us something you remember from up here. Something you liked," James says.

"I remember the day before they offered us the chance to go underground. I met this beautiful brunette at this bar on Lincoln Avenue—the Tiki Lounge. It was one of those Hawaiian-themed rooms. She was there by herself. Most of her family had been killed in the big quake, just like mine, but she was still smiling somehow, like an angel. I bought her a drink and asked her to dance."

"Dance?" Bones says. "Is that slang for *bang*?"

"No, man. We just danced. She had the softest skin I've ever felt and her hair was so shiny. I remember the lights just getting lost in her hair, as did my eyes. She was beautiful. That night in the bar, that was the last time I saw her. And even after all the women I've slept with over the years, I still think about her. The one who got away."

Bones, Reeko, and James smile, their eyes looking off into another world, another time, but then James' smile turns to a frown. "Do you guys think there's *anyone* left up here?"

"Who could survive up here?" Reeko says.

"*What* could survive up here?" Chop adds.

Bones shakes his head. "I know there's something up here."

"How?" Chop says. "We were up here working years ago. Nobody found anything."

"No. I can feel them." Bones looks at row after row of window cutouts on a building. "There's something up here, watching us. I know it."

"What the hell did they put in your chicken?" Reeko says.

Chop and Bones laugh.

James stares at the building. A light flickers inside a window, but after he blinks, it's gone.

The Rover speeds past the building toward an open field.

Bones sees the red dot approaching on his navigation system. "We're a hundred yards away," he says as they speed forty miles an hour.

They reach a steep descent. "Hold on!" Bones shouts.

The Rover shudders down the hill. One of the packs gets loose so James reaches to secure it.

They speed through the open area.

"Where the hell is the river?" Chop asks.

"We're inside it," James says.

Chop sees the hill they had just descended, the edge of the river.

"The only water left is the supply from the bedrock," James says. "That's all that's left."

"The drinking water for the rich," Reeko says.

Up ahead is a shell of a submarine. A rectangle with one star of the American flag still etches the side.

The Rover zips forward, and then Bones lets up, coasting it.

"Where the hell is this bridge?" Reeko says.

Bones stops the Rover. They sit in the middle of the vast riverbed. The orange sky strengthens as they search the area.

"It says the bridge is right here," Bones says, seeing their location on the navigation system.

"There's no bridge here," Chop says.

"No, shit," Reeko goes. "That navigation system is busted. I can't believe they gave us a *busted* machine."

"It's gotta be here," Bones says.

"Open your eyes!" Reeko shouts. "There's no bridge here!"

"Maybe somebody came down and took it," Chop says.

"Took a two-mile bridge?" Reeko says. "Did aliens use the tow hitch on their space ship? That system is jacked up. These suits are probably jacked up too. This is a fuckin' joke."

James sees a reflection fifty yards away. "Go further up."

Bones moves the Rover forward.

"There's nothing above us for miles," Reeko says.

James sees reflecting metal on the side of the riverbank. "Not above us. Over there, on the side."

The metal reflects eighty yards away on the side of the bank. Bones navigates the Rover toward it. He comes up to the side of the river. "We're going up."

The Rover accelerates and ascends the hill, the guys rocking in their seats.

"Here we go again!" Bones shouts.

They launch over the top, going airborne five feet into the air. Then they come down hard, bouncing off their seats.

"Over there. See," James says.

Bones speeds toward the metal. It's a portion of the bridge. A dozen suspension cables reach for the sky. Thirty yards of support beams extend from the river edge.

The Rover stops nearby.

"There it is," Chop says.

Bones squints his eyes. "But where's the rest of it?"

Reeko looks at James through his visor, fear in his eyes. Chop and Bones turn around and stare at their mates. The idle of the Rover flows through them.

James takes a deep breath and sees his suit's oxygen level go from "80%" to "79%."

"Where's the rest of the bridge?" Chop says. "I thought we were going to use this to keep sustaining the shields."

"I can't answer that. We're here to do a job," Reeko says. "Do we have enough to harvest for today?"

James sees the cross support beams and sheets of metal. "I think so. We can get what we need from there."

Bones speeds the Rover to the remnants of the bridge. He kills the engine, and then presses a button on the dashboard. The trailer door lowers from the back and locks into place.

"Let's get to work," Reeko says.

The guys jump out of the Rover.

Chop takes a deep breath and whispers, "Where the hell did the bridge go?"

29

The sight of a gun aims at a black silhouette. It sways over the chest of the target.

Pop!

A muffled shot hits the 90 mark. Melissa lowers the silenced pistol.

"Not bad. Not bad," Lance says, wearing his UVASHIELD polo shirt.

Philip comes into the lab room. "You can hear the shots out here."

"Any military?" Melissa asks.

"They're having a meeting in the common area."

"Probably their escape plan," Lance says.

Melissa squeezes the gun. "All we need is a pilot and we can do this."

"I'll go get him, ma'am. And meet you at the chopper," Lance says.

Melissa nods. "Okay. Twenty minutes. We tell the military that we're collecting sensor data."

"You ever shoot?" Lance asks Philip.

He turns red. "Me? No, I don't like guns. I don't need one."

"How are you going to defend yourself?" Lance says.

"He's just going because of his persuasive personality," Melissa says. "He'll get us into the New White House."

Lance raises his pistol. "Well, this is my *persuasive personality*."

"Twenty minutes at the chopper," Melissa says, looking at her smart tablet.

Philip checks outside the door and sees the empty corridor. He nods at Melissa, who nods back. Philip leaves first and goes left.

Melissa puts the pistol and her smart tablet into her briefcase. She nods at Lance, and then leaves to the right down the corridor.

A young military man stands guard in front of the common area. He looks at Melissa's sway, and then at the briefcase in her hand.

She ignores him and stares at the UVASHIELD logo at the end of the hallway. After zigzagging through the corridors, she enters her suite.

Alex, Brian, and Janice stand up from the table.

Richard watches her enter. "What'd you find out?"

She starts coughing fiercely so Alex hands her some water.

"Sit down," Richard says, patting her back.

Melissa sits down at the table.

"Are you okay?" Janice asks.

"Well, Lance from security is on board. Philip and I will meet him with the pilot at the chopper in eighteen minutes."

"I want to go too to see this snake," Janice says, her eyes narrow.

"We must do this smart," Melissa says. She opens her briefcase and removes her bottle of yellow liquid.

Alex sees the gun. "Is that a gun, Mom?"

"It's just for protection," Melissa replies as she takes a swig of the medicine without measuring it.

"If you're walking into a trap, you're better off here," Richard says.

"No, it's our only chance. Philip has some connections there at the New White House. I don't think Secretary Dunner could have paid off all of the government. This is the only way."

Brian hands her a quarter. "Here, Mrs. Mercer. Take this, for good luck."

She accepts the quarter and stares at the image of George Washington. The date says, "2013."

"Where did you get this?" Melissa asks.

"My dad gave it to me. He got it up on the surface before I was born."

Melissa stands up and hugs Brian, squeezing him with life, with love. "Thank you."

Richard gives her a bottle of water and puts his hands on her shoulders. "I love you, honey. You are so smart. We'll be here for you."

"We're going to see our son and his friend grow up," she says. Then she kisses him. "I love you too."

Melissa goes to the door and starts coughing.

"Is she going to be okay?" Janice asks.

"She's a strong woman," Richard replies.

Melissa moves down the corridor. Up ahead, two military men laugh. Melissa slows down and bites her lip, but continues toward the men.

"That chic with the big tits is down there in suite Ten A," one says.

"You're not getting my ticket to save her," the other one says.

When Melissa approaches, one of the men wipes the sweat on the back of his neck. She grips the briefcase even tighter.

"Badge, ma'am," the one with the deep voice says.

Melissa shows them her UVASHIELD badge while staring at a crack in the floor. She makes it past them. A sign reads, "Landing Deck – Right."

"That broad looks like a zombie," the higher-pitched military man says behind her.

She moves toward the right. The heat punches her face, enough to slow her steps. She takes a deep breath; the smell of sewage enters her lungs.

Four steps from the doorway to the landing deck, a shadow shifts on her side. "Mrs. Mercer, where are you going?"

The voice is thick, raw, like a hot wind through the sweltering desert. The choppers are only twenty yards away through the doorway, but before she can reach them, the shadow turns into the colonel and blocks her way.

"Hey, where are you going?" he says, looking at her briefcase.

Melissa keeps her eyes on the choppers. "Do you feel that heat? We need to check the thermal units on each turbine."

"Where's your authorization form?"

"Authorization form?" she says, looking at the colonel.

"The Secretary of Defense has enacted martial law. Every flight needs proper clearance."

"Your men are feeling the effects of the heat already. I know most of them got tickets. If they get heat exhaustion, how are they going to make it to quadrant two before seven o'clock tonight? We'll be back shortly."

The colonel looks into her eyes and slithers through her brain, trying to find the truth.

Melissa starts coughing.

"Did you get a ticket?" the colonel asks.

She wipes her cheek with her suit jacket. "Did *I* get a ticket?" she says. "Just look around you. This is my business, my life. What do you think?"

"Mrs. Mercer, is there a problem?" Lance says from inside the doorway. He marches their way, his hand behind his back.

Melissa widens her eyes at Lance. "This is my security escort, Colonel. We'll be up and back before you know it. I'm bringing one of my support staff. He can fix the units. It'll make it more comfortable for your men."

The colonel scratches his chin. "Captain Miller," he shouts.

A tall man with slicked hair comes over. "Yes, sir."

"Take bird two and escort Mrs. Mercer. She's going to try to cool it off down here."

"Yes, sir," Captain Miller says.

Melissa looks at Lance and exhales. They meet Philip near the chopper.

Lance gives the pilot a thumbs up. The pilot enables the engine.

"What's going on?" Philip whispers.

"We have a tail now," she says, gesturing to Captain Miller entering a camouflaged chopper. Another army guy jumps inside as Captain Miller engages the rotating blades.

"*This* is why we need guns," Lance says.

30

Sparks fly into the air. James kneels and uses the fire from a torch to cut through the metal. He presses against the piece to loosen it. "This is some tough shit."

"That's a good thing," Reeko says, trying to support the piece.

Bones and Chop load sheets of metal into the trailer.

James keeps the flame against the metal, sparks showering over him.

Reeko screams, pushing the piece to break it free.

The flame cuts through the last connection, and then the piece falls down.

James kills the fire and sits down, sweat covering his face. He reads his heads-up display: "External Temperature: 214, Internal Temperature: 92, Oxygen Level: 61%."

"Take a break, brother," Chop says. "This heat is making my moustache droop."

"I'll rest when I'm in quadrant two with my family," James says.

Chop and Bones pick up the fallen piece.

"What's your O2?" Reeko asks.

"I'm at sixty-one," James says.

"I'm still at seventy-four," Reeko says. "Let me do this for a while. You're going to be empty with all that heavy breathing." Reeko grabs the torch.

"All that breathing, they're going to think you're masturbating in there," Chop says.

They all laugh.

Reeko enables the flame and angles it toward another piece of metal.

James stands up and beholds a five-foot pile of steel sheets. He uses his eyes to select "Hydration" from the menu. A straw comes down and he sucks up liquid.

James looks around at the wide-open space made of gravel and stone. Shells of the skyscrapers stand tall in the distance. The piece of bridge is the only thing left as the void extends over the riverbed.

A flicker of light catches James' eye a hundred feet above them on top of the piece of bridge. He moves a few feet and looks up at the suspension cables reaching for the orange sky.

"Are you looking for the stars?" Bones says.

"I saw something up there."

"Go take a break in the shade," Chop says, gesturing to the shady part under the bridge.

James moves toward Chop's gesture, stepping through the sparks. When he sits down, he sees something round buried in the dirt.

It's a Campbell's soup can.

A metal spoon is inside. James turns the can over. Liquid dumps out and boils into steam once it hits the ground.

James digs deeper and discovers two more soup cans and a can of sardines, each containing a fork. He stands up. "Hey, Chop. Come here."

"You just pee, brother. The suit sucks it up," Chop says.

"No, you gotta see this."

Chop leaves the Rover as Bones picks up two ten-inch pieces of metal and secures them in the trailer.

James uncovers four more cans.

"What'd you got?" Chop says.

"Look at this stuff."

"They're just old cans, probably buried down there and protected in the ground."

Juice pours out of the sardine can when James turns it over. "These don't look old to me."

"What are you idiots doing over here?" Bones says.

The light flickers above them so they look up.

Something on top of the bridge moves.

James' heart stops. Chop freezes stiff. Bones holds his breath.

Another flicker catches their eyes.

James squints but the light is too bright. The suit tries to compensate by darkening the visor. He looks at the edge of the bridge.

A tall creature looks down at them. It's shaped like a human with red, fleshy tissue. It's hairless, lanky, its arms and legs as thin as bones.

Below the creature is Reeko, engrossed in the flames from the blowtorch.

The creature looks at James for a split second and grips his soul with pain, with rage, with violence.

197

"Reeko!" James yells.

The creature dives onto Reeko, knocking him back.

"Get it!" Bones shouts.

The three guys run over.

The creature pounces on Reeko.

Flames from the torch fire into the air.

Reeko pushes the creature down, but it hisses and lashes at his suit.

"Get the emergency pouch!" James shouts.

Chop runs toward the Rover.

White smoke escapes from Reeko's suit. He grabs the blowtorch and sends flames into the abdomen of the creature. It keeps its force and attacks the suit.

As James and Bones approach the creature, it stops and stares at them, a bomb ready to explode.

Chop opens the pack and grabs the extinguisher. He sprays it toward Reeko, some hitting the creature. It shrieks and jumps onto the rail of the bridge and climbs up.

Reeko flails his arms. His O2 level drops from 10%, down to 8%, down to 6%.

"Let me see your suit!" James shouts, but Reeko scampers. "Keep him cool!"

Chop sprays the suit, but Reeko keeps moving. He kicks up the blowtorch as fire sprays at Bones. Reeko nears the edge of the riverbank.

"Reeko! No!" James yells, diving toward him.

Reeko goes over the edge.

James reaches for him, his suit touching Reeko's.

For a moment, they lock eyes. James sees tears glossing the eyes of his coworker, his friend. And then Reeko falls down, toppling over and over and over. He plummets a hundred feet, the suit breaking open. His body flies out and bursts into flames.

Finally, Reeko comes to a rest at the bottom of the river.

"Reeko!" Bones shouts.

The three men peer over the edge and witness the lifeless, burning body.

Bones stands up and throws a piece of metal up at the bridge. "Goddamn! Show yourself!"

James nearly spills over, but Chop pulls him back from the edge. "They got Reeko!" Chop shouts. "They got Reeko!"

James shakes his head.

Chop's stomach sinks. "His body. We got to get him."

James and Chop see the raging fire below them.

James closes his eyes. "He's gone. There's nothing we can do now."

"What the hell was that thing?" Chop says.

James looks up at the bridge, and then at the Rover. "How many emergency pouches do we have?"

"Three more," Chop says.

"Come back down here!" Bones shouts.

"Bones! Bones!" James says, grabbing him. "Stop it, man."

"Let's fight this fucker."

"We can't stay here," James says. "We have a job to do."

"Job? Fuck the job!"

Chop comes over and puts his hand on Bone's back, but he flicks him off.

"You want to fight them?" James says. "Let's fight them, but let's keep working."

"Who put *you* in charge?" Bones stops moving and calms down. "He's gone. Reeko's fuckin' gone."

James sees the metal on the back of the Rover. "Do we have enough steel?"

"Yeah, I think," Chop says.

"Let's get this last piece and get the hell out of here." James goes to the Rover and checks the other emergency pouches. He opens them and removes the extinguishers. He hands one each to Bones and Chop. "They don't like these."

"*They*?" Chop says. "You think there are more?"

"I hope there are more so I can send them all to hell," Bones says.

James clutches his extinguisher. "Maybe we're already in hell."

31

Captain Miller appears down the sight of a pistol. The gun sways between him and the co-pilot in the front seat, and then it locks onto the chest of Captain Miller.

"Boom," Lance says, pretending to pull the trigger.

Melissa and Philip face Lance as their pilot commands the chopper.

"That won't work," Philip says. "The bullet will be rattling around inside here."

Melissa shakes her head. "I'm not going to revert to violence unless *absolutely* necessary."

"It's every man for themselves, ma'am," Lance says.

"It doesn't even matter," she says. "We have the army following us."

Lance raises his gun. "Let's bring this down and have a good ol' fashioned shootout."

"Where there's one chopper, there are others," Melissa says. "But you *might* be on to something."

Lance bites the corner of his lip. "With what?"

"Bring us down," Melissa says.

Philip looks down at the tracks on the long concrete corridor. "There's just a train corridor below us, ma'am."

"Take us to quadrant four," Melissa says to the pilot.

"Four? That's in total chaos, ma'am," the pilot says, looking into Melissa's eyes.

Confidence stares back at him.

The chopper speeds down the corridor and banks toward a passage on the right.

The military chopper banks quickly and tails Melissa's chopper with ease.

A ten-foot sign displays, "Quadrant 4 – Next Right."

The UVASHIELD chopper follows the sign.

The military chopper speeds alongside Melissa's helicopter. Captain Miller holds up his smart tablet to the window. Written on it is "Tune to 103."

The pilot adjusts his radio. "This is UVASHIELD One. Go ahead." He looks over and nods at Captain Miller. "Roger that."

The pilot gives a headset to Melissa. "This is Melissa Mercer."

"Where are you going? Quadrant four is not connected to us in quadrant five."

"The thermal units are all in a linked system," she says. "When one goes down, they all go down. Just like Christmas tree lights."

Captain Miller shakes his head. "Okay, let us lead the way."

Melissa takes off the headset as the military chopper propels in front.

"Now it's the blind leading the blind," Philip says.

The bay door for quadrant four approaches. The military chopper reaches the entryway first. As the door opens, smoke billows out.

The UVASHIELD chopper follows the military helicopter inside. A bottle hits the glass next to Melissa. She winces.

Smoke swirls in the air. Heat blasts the chopper.

Melissa takes off her suit jacket.

People shout and hold signs that read, "We're not Rats!" and "The lottery is fixed!" A barricade with a single entry point protects military men and workers in front of a sign that displays, "Get your lottery ticket here. Fingerprint Verification Required." A hundred people shake the fence, trying to get in.

The smell of sewage attacks the chopper.

Melissa covers her nose with her jacket, but the smell of sweat in the fabric causes her to dry-heave.

The mob looks up at the choppers.

Melissa connects eyes with a grizzly man.

He points at her. The people start throwing stones and refuse at the choppers.

"Is this a good idea?" Lance says as they weave around the projectiles.

"Where to?" Captain Miller says in the headset.

"The turbines up ahead and on the right. There's a landing zone."

"Landing zone? That's a negative. It's too hot."

"Your job is to protect us, Captain Miller," Melissa says. "So protect us."

The military chopper rockets a hundred yards in front, leaving the mob behind.

Melissa sees the busted windows, cracked tables, and broken chairs at the Ghost Bar. Vendor carts are toppled over. She recognizes the skull tattoo on the back of a scrawny guy; his abdomen is sunken even further into his ribcage. He bites the head off a rat and looks up at Melissa, stealing her breath.

The four turbines are in front of them. Only two are turning.

"No wonder it's really bad here," Philip says. "Only two are working. Aren't those the ones that the crew on the surface tried fixing?"

Melissa sees the open landing area. "Bring us down here."

Both choppers land. Only a few stragglers line the area of the quadrant.

"What's the plan?" Lance says.

Melissa looks at the mob a hundred yards away encroaching on their area. "Keep the blades spinning. Get ready to take us up."

Lance jumps out and cocks his pistol.

Melissa and Philip step out.

Captain Miller and the other army guy meet them.

"The area is hot. How long is this going to take?" Captain Miller says, gripping his submachine gun.

"Just keep us safe," Melissa says. She goes over to the wall and looks up at the turbine units.

"What exactly are we doing?" Lance says.

"The pigeonhole principle," she replies.

"I don't get it."

"Those two military guys are the holes. And there are about two hundred pigeons coming to plug the holes." Melissa inserts a cable from her smart tablet into a port on the wall. The screen shows, "Downloading Data." She smirks. "It's been a long time since I've done this."

"This is why we have grunts," Philip says.

Melissa looks into his eyes. "Never forget where you came from, Philip."

The screen shows, "Internal Temp: 95. Turbines One and Three Offline."

"It's ninety-five in here?" Philip says.

"But it's a dry heat," Lance says.

"Let's go!" Captain Miller shouts. "We gotta get airborne."

The crazed people are only thirty yards away, and their screams hurl toward them.

"I'm going back to the chopper," Philip says.

"No! Wait!" Melissa unplugs the smart tablet.

Lance clutches his gun. "I'm drawing my weapon."

"I said wait!"

"Back in the choppers!" Captain Miller yells.

Melissa connects eyes with the scrawny guy. She nods toward the military chopper.

"There!" the scrawny guy screams, directing the mob toward the military chopper.

"Okay. Let's move," Melissa shouts, leading the way to her chopper.

The mob surrounds the camouflaged bird. People throw stones. Some ricochet off the blades toward Philip. He grabs onto Lance.

Captain Miller jumps on the landing gear of the chopper. The co-pilot pulls the trigger on the chopper's machine guns. Bullets blast the crowd, tearing through the flesh of the men and women.

"Whoa!" Philip shouts.

Melissa dives into her chopper as Lance pushes Philip inside.

Captain Miller runs to help his comrade, but the scrawny guy pounces on him. People jump inside the military chopper.

"Go up!" Melissa says. "Go up!"

205

"You're doing the devil's work!" The grubby old man with the scars reaches in and grabs Philip.

Philip screams and hangs off the side of the chopper. "Help!"

The chopper wavers as it ascends.

Philip slides out further.

A glass bottle smashes inches from Philip's head.

Lance pulls him up.

The grubby old man falls back into the mob as the chopper climbs.

The military chopper bobbles. The mob consumes Captain Miller and his co-pilot. People hang off the side as the chopper rises up.

"They're going to blow themselves up!" Lance shouts.

A man jumps on the pilot inside the military chopper and steers toward the wall fifty yards away. The blades hit the wall first, and then the body. The chopper ignites into a fireball.

The explosion rocks the quadrant as the fireworks incite the people.

Melissa holds on.

"Do you think they felt it back in quadrant five?" Philip says.

Melissa stares at the fire. "I think they felt it everywhere."

32

The Rover hops up three feet in the air. Three sheets of steel fall off the trailer.

"What the hell was that?" Chop says.

James turns around and sees the fallen steel. "Hold it!"

Bones slows the Rover to a stop.

James jumps off and runs back.

"Was that an earthquake?" Chop says.

Bones goes out and glances at Chop. "You keep any eye out for those things."

Chop stands guard with his extinguisher, staring at a half arc of a mangled Ferris wheel fifty yards away.

Bones and James drag the three pieces to the trailer.

"Let's lift on three," James says.

"One...two...*three*." They strain to lift one of the sheets up, tossing it onto the pile.

Chop moves toward them. "Let me help."

"No. I'm not letting those things sneak up on us," Bones says.

Bones and James repeat the process for the second sheet.

"What the hell do you think they are?" Chop asks.

"Monsters," Bones says.

"Seriously though," Chop says.

They finish lifting the third piece and secure the metal with a tie.

James looks at Chop. "I don't know. Some sort of mutated creature. Who knows what the radiation and the UV light have done. Remember when we went underground. How did you get down there?"

"I was just going to see if they had work on this side of the city. Then, next thing I know there were military guys offering us a chance to go to the underground bunkers. I didn't think they'd built a city."

"How about you Bones?" James says.

"I don't want to talk," he replies, tightening the cables.

"The same thing with me," James says. "I was just at the right place at the right time. We were all the lucky ones."

"Were we?" Bones says.

"On Underground Day, I was fifteen, alone, and giving up on this world. Now I have a wife, a son."

"What the fuck do I have?" Bones says. "I used to have a friend, but now he's lying at the bottom of a riverbed burned to a crisp."

"Hey, I have a shit life too," Chop says. "We're doing this for the survivors."

Bones slams his hand down on the steel. "Fuck the survivors."

"Let's not do this now," James says. "Let's just worry about work."

"Easy for you to say, selfish prick," Bones says.

James narrows his eyes. "Hey, watch your mouth."

"What're you going to do, huh?" Bones storms toward James, his fist clenched.

"Guys! Over there," Chop shouts.

Fifty yards in the distance, two burned creatures stare at them, their eyes reflecting.

"Let's get out of here," Chop says, returning to the front seat of the Rover.

Bones rushes to the driver's seat.

"Wait," James says.

Bones and Chop look at the creatures.

"What are they doing?" Chop says.

James stretches his neck. "Isn't that a shield over there?"

Bones checks the navigation system. "Yeah, we're actually right over quadrant four. That's probably the shield for that busted turbine unit we have to keep fixing."

Suddenly, the creatures scurry away toward a burned-out building.

Chop's heart flutters. "They're leaving."

"Let's spin over there quick," James says.

Bones shakes his head. "We're not fixing quadrant four. You keep preaching about doing the job."

"I know," James says. "But it'll take two minutes. Go over there...please."

Bones exhales. He kicks it into gear and drives toward the shield. "Alright, man. But I'm down to sixty percent on my oxygen."

"I'm at fifty-two," James says.

The Rover shakes over gravel and rock. They move around the mangled metal of the Ferris wheel.

Chop keeps his eyes on the burned-out building a hundred yards away, his hands clutching the extinguisher.

They approach a twenty-foot-by-twenty-foot structure. A box of layered steel sits on top of the opening with vents around the base. The UVASHIELD logo is plastered on the side.

The Rover stops. The hum of the turbines under the shield filters through the area.

James steps out and walks toward the structure. The metal on top of the covering is withered. There's a hole the size of a basketball in the center. Deep scratches cut through the U and the V of the logo.

James kneels down and rubs the dust off the metal. The scratches extend across the top of the shield. His eyes widen as his heart pounds in his chest.

He runs back to the cart. "Let's go."

Bones puts it into gear and speeds away.

"What'd you find?" Chop asks.

"You know how they said the sudden temperature rise has been weakening the shields?"

"Yeah," Chop says.

"That's not the only thing weakening the shields. Those *things* are clawing at them."

"Shit," Chop says. "No wonder the turbines keep breaking. They're fucking with the airflow balance."

"Let's get the bastards," Bones says.

James squeezes his eyes shut, pain gripping his brain. "With what weapons? A couple of cans of extinguisher? Those are supposed to be for us. And who knows how many there are?"

"Why would they want to claw at the shields?" Bones says.

"Who knows?" James replies. "Maybe they want to come down with us."

"Or not want us down there," Bones says. He launches them over a sand dune.

They hold on as the Rover comes down hard, the trailer rattling.

"Slow it down, man," Chop says.

"How much farther to our destination?" James asks.

Bones keeps the throttle pegged.

"Bones!" James shouts, but Bones ignores him. The Rover continues to speed faster and faster.

A large dune is up ahead.

"Slow down!" Chop yells.

"Stop!" James screams, grabbing Bones' shoulder.

Bones lets up on the throttle and coasts the Rover. He turns to go around the dune. The Rover comes to a stop, and then sits idling.

"What the hell's wrong with you?" Chop says.

Bones rests his head down on the steering wheel. "I need a drink. Something strong."

"Let's finish this first," James says.

"He was right there in front of us, man," Bones lifts his head up and punches the steering wheel. "Why did we leave him alone? Those damn things came from nowhere. I shouldn't have left him alone."

James and Chop remain silent. They all just sit and listen to the idling engine.

The orange intensifies around them. The vastness of the open area spreads for miles, the cityscape ten miles in front of them.

James licks his crusty lips and checks his heads-up display. The external temperature reads, "217." The internal temperature shows, "95." James selects the hydration menu and sucks up some fluid. The menu beeps and displays, "Warning – 20% remaining hydration." His oxygen reads, "50%."

The Rover starts moving.

"Where are we going?" James says.

Bones points at the red dot on the screen. "To reinforce the shields."

Chop pats him on the back as they continue forward.

Miles rack up as silence consumes the Rover. James stares at the scorched cars on the sides of the roads.

The Rover reaches the city streets and rolls with authority.

Buildings pass by. Bones steers around the frame of an airplane. They pass the same tank from when they had entered.

James checks the trailer behind him, but a flicker from one of the buildings distracts him. He faces forward and grips the seat even tighter.

The red dot approaches on the navigation system.

"Five more miles," Bones says.

The skyscrapers thin out. They jet into an area with a pile-up of cars, now just shells of metal.

A forty-foot sinkhole is at the end of an open area. Bones steers around it.

In front of them, a chain-link fence still stands.

"Hold on," Bones says.

The Rover plows through it.

Row after row of stones form a grid. The Rover speeds over them with ease.

A hill is in front of them. Bones accelerates the Rover as the stones become larger. He tries to steer around them as they speed up the hill.

Something pops. The Rover jostles. Packs fly off. Bones hits the brakes, but the trailer jackknifes before coming to a stop.

"Is everyone okay?" James says.

"Yeah," Bones replies.

"What the hell just happened?" Chop says.

Bones jumps off. "Punctured tire."

James gets out and looks at the jagged stone twenty yards back. The steel is still in the trailer. He checks the tire and sees a gouge in the sidewall.

"Where are we?" Chop asks.

James kneels down in front of one of the stones and wipes the dust off. He sees, "Randolph Malhalshick 1929 – 2001."

"We're stuck in a fuckin' cemetery?" Chop says, looking around at the rows of tombstones.

Two twenty-foot-wide tomb lockers still stand fifty yards away.

James opens a compartment in the back of the Rover and finds a new tire. "I'll change it. Bones, you help. Chop, you pick up the packs, and then stand guard." James grabs the jack. "Just like my dad's Chevy." He attaches it to the frame and starts jacking.

Chop grabs the pack. On the ground, he sees the face of a woman engraved on a tombstone.

Something flickers in the corner of his eye.

He looks at the tomb lockers; only the color orange from the sky hangs in the air.

Bones lifts the spare tire and balances it on the ground, waiting for James.

James removes the busted tire and exchanges it with Bones.

As Bones waits, he notices a row of tombstones without sand on their faces. One of them reads, "Edward Jouris, 1938 – 20." Dust covers the last two digits.

He steps toward the stone, slowly, curiously. Suddenly, the ground opens. He falls down hard, his leg twisting. "Help!"

James and Chop rush to the edge of the sinkhole.

Bones is six feet in the Earth.

"Hang in there!" James shouts.

"My leg!" Bones screams.

A hissing sound expels from his suit. Bones sees his oxygen level dropping, "55%...54%...53%..." The internal temperature rises, hitting 100.

James points at the eight-foot rod in the trailer. "Grab that piece of steel," James says to Chop. "Hang in there, Bones!"

"I can't breathe!"

Chop and James lower the rod into the hole. "Grab this. We'll pull you up," James says.

Bones grabs the end of the rod.

James and Chop pull, grunting and struggling.

Bones rises up. His leg is twisted and gas escapes through the gash in his suit.

James and Chop pull him out. "You're okay," James says. He looks at Bones' leg, which is twisted below his hip. "Get the repair kit in the emergency pouch," James says to Chop.

Gas shoots out. James covers it with his hand, but it escapes through his fingers.

Chop removes a roll of green tape labeled, "Sealant – Temporary use only." He unravels it and wraps Bones' leg.

The hissing stops. Inside, the temperature stops rising at 104, and then drops down to 97. The oxygen stabilizes at 22%.

James assesses Bones' twisted leg. "Does this hurt?" he asks, trying to straighten it.

"Ouch! Yeah, it fuckin' hurts."

James moves it back.

"Ouch! Watch it!"

"Let's get him back into the Rover."

James and Chop grab his shoulders to help him up, his leg dangling.

"Ow! Ow! My leg!"

They plop him down into the backseat.

"Goddamn!" Bones shouts.

Chop sees a flicker near the tombs. He studies the stone structures, but then makes out the long arms and legs, the seared flesh, the evil glare of a creature.

"Shit!" Chop says. "There's one of those things."

"Hurry. Hurry. Let's go." James drops down in front of the tire and tightens the bolts.

The creature runs toward them, getting closer and closer and closer.

Chop jumps into the driver's seat and starts the engine, his breathing chaotic.

"Hurry! It's coming!" Bones grabs the extinguisher from the pouch next to him.

Heart pounding, James finishes the tire and dives into the front passenger seat.

The creature is ten yards away, running like a track star.

Chop hits the throttle, launching them forward.

The creature leaps into the air and lands in the trailer. It hangs on as Chop speeds them up the hill.

Bones sprays a shot of the extinguisher, but misses.

The creature looks into Bones' eyes and opens its mouth, shrieking, the sound snaking down their spines.

The Rover reaches the top of the hill.

The creature dives through the air toward Bones. He pulls the extinguisher and a blast of CO_2 hits the creature. It screeches and rolls back off the trailer and down the hill.

The terrain levels off, the hill now a half mile in the distance.

"Are you guys okay?" James says.

Chop clutches the steering wheel. "Scared shitless."

Bones listens to the sound of the pain screaming in his body. "Fuck, my leg."

James looks at the navigation system. "Let's bring you back underground."

"No. No. Just go, man. It's too far. I'm fucked." Bones sees his O2 level at "14%."

33

Coffee steams inside a cup on the table. The book is open and a bite is missing from the turkey sandwich.

Melissa sits up. She sees the bags from Victoria's Secret next to the young women at the adjacent table.

Traffic flows through the street. People walk.

Melissa takes a deep breath. The taxicab is further down the street. She gets up, knocks over the chair, and jumps over the railing.

The man, Richard, wheels the baby carriage. Melissa runs to him.

A tremor rocks the area and steals everyone's focus.

Melissa reaches him as the big quake grips the city. She sees a clothing store in front of them.

Cars wreck. People scream. The taxi races toward them.

Melissa pushes Richard inside, but the carriage breaks free. It rolls toward the street, toward the path of the speeding taxi.

The ground opens.

Melissa stumbles toward the carriage as the taxi impales it. Her body hits the front of the taxi, the tires rolling over her legs, crushing them.

She's pinned under the vehicle with the carriage.

Baby Alex cries.

Melissa crawls to him, her legs mangled. She reaches the carriage, but it's empty. She looks further under the taxi and sees a ten-inch-wide hole into the Earth, a hole wide enough for her baby.

Inside, her baby falls toward the void, his cries fading away to nothing.

The taxi bursts into flames. Melissa's body catches fire, the heat so intense it's beyond heat.

"Mrs. Mercer! Can you hear me?" a voice shouts as if it's underwater.

The fire is too intense.

Beyond the dream world housing Melissa's mind, her body sits deep beneath the planet Earth, flying inside a helicopter.

Philip stands over her lifeless body. "Mrs. Mercer. Mrs. Mercer. Can you hear me?"

Lance looks in her pack and finds the prescription bottle of liquid. "What's this?"

"It's what she's been taking. She's been sick lately, fainting and vomiting. It must be the stress."

"And the heat," Lance says. "Here, open her mouth. We'll put some under her tongue."

"Do you want me to turn back?" the pilot asks.

"Negative," Lance says. "We're almost there. Stick to the plan."

Through the thick heat miles away, a wafer sits in the center of a table.

Richard breaks off a piece, sweat dripping from his beard. He places the piece in front of Alex, who rests his head on the table, his hair slicked with perspiration. Janice and Brian sit next to each other at the table, their clothes drenched with sweat.

"You guys should eat some," Richard says.

"Thank you," Janice replies, the heat slowing her smile.

"It's too hot," Brian says.

"I know, baby. Just eat. You'll need your strength when we go to quadrant two."

"We're not going. We're going to burn up down here."

Janice swallows. "Hey now. Don't talk like that."

"Dad," Alex says. "When it gets so hot, will we burn into fire? Is it going to hurt?"

Richard pushes his cup of water in front of Alex. "Take a sip, buddy, and then give some to Brian."

"We can't drink it all," Janice says. "You haven't had anything."

Richard raises his hand a few inches off the table. "I'll be fine."

Janice shakes her head. "Now you sound like your wife."

Richard goes to smile, but hesitates, and turns it into a frown.

Miles through the underground labyrinth, the chopper speeds through the sweltering heat. It approaches a sign, "Entering the New White House."

"We're almost there," the pilot says, seeing the control room up ahead.

Philip cradles Melissa's head and combs her hair with his fingers. He sees her chest rising and the subtle thumps in the artery in her neck. He leans down and whispers into her ear. "Wake up, Mrs. Mercer. Richard and Alex are counting on you."

Melissa's eyes open. She starts coughing.

Lance helps her sit forward to ease her cough.

"The bay door is up here," the pilot says, watching the military guards pacing the catwalk.

A voice fills their headsets, "UVASHIELD chopper. This is NWH control. Identify your approach. I repeat—identify your approach."

Melissa calms down.

"Mrs. Mercer, just breathe," Philip says. "We are here at the New White House. To save the president."

She sits up.

The chopper slows down and hovers outside the closed door, the turrets twenty yards away.

"Can we ram this sucker?" Lance says.

"We're not in a tank," the pilot replies.

"UVASHIELD chopper. Identify your approach. This is your last warning."

Melissa stoops down and moves to the front. "I'm okay now."

"How are we going to get in?" Philip asks.

"Your friend, the chief of staff. Ask for him," Melissa says.

Philip blushes. "I'm not good at lying."

"You don't have to sleep with him," Melissa says, handing him the headset.

Philip puts it on and presses the button to talk. "Yes, I have the CEO of UVASHIELD here. We have an appointment with Ross Barkston."

"We don't have any appointment in our binder."

"Can you please call him? He is expecting us. Tell him it's Philip from UVASHIELD regarding the ICU plan."

"It's like David versus Goliath," Lance whispers.

"Ross Barkston is not here," the soldier says through the headset. "He's probably with his family preparing to leave."

Melissa shakes her head.

Lance cocks his weapon. "Goddamn. Let me off over there. We'll do this old school."

"Uh, UVASHIELD chopper, you are cleared. Please proceed through and take bay twelve."

The bay door opens.

Philip, Melissa, and Lance look at each other with narrowed eyes.

"Roger that," the pilot says.

"Why would they let us in?" Philip says.

Lance connects eyes with the soldier in the control room. "Wait. I'm not walking into a trap."

"We don't know this is a trap. We must try," Melissa says.

The chopper floats slowly through the door.

A half-dozen military choppers are parked in bays. The lights shine brightly. The heat is strong. The smell of the sewer loiters. Only one out of the four turbines spins.

Melissa wipes her face. "Even the New White House can't hide from the heat."

The pilot brings the chopper down in bay 12.

"What do we do?" Philip asks.

"We storm that door over there," Lance says. "You know the inside. Let's find this fucker."

"Hey, we're not jumping into the fire so fast," Melissa says.

The chopper spins down.

Philip opens the side door. Lance and Melissa step out.

The area is lifeless. The only movements are the eyes of the three mice approaching the mouth of the cat.

"Let's go," Melissa says.

"Where is everyone?" Philip whispers.

"It's too quiet," Lance says, checking his pistol on the holster under his shirt.

Suddenly, two military men emerge from the door. They wear stone faces, eyes detached from the world, fingers resting on the triggers of their assault weapons. One has orange skin and the other has a thick neck.

"Where have you been?" the tanned one says.

"What?" Melissa replies.

"The heat is unbearable. Those turbines have been down for a while."

"Uh, yeah, we've been checking the thermal units. It could be something simple."

"Why is the CEO of the company coming to check thermal units?" the thick guy says.

Lance feels his weapon.

Philip puts his head down.

Melissa stands tall. "Sometimes the boss needs to get her hands dirty."

"Where do you have to go?" the tanned guard asks.

"All of the units. We'll start at cabinet member offices. We just need to get our tools."

Melissa leads Philip and Lance back to the chopper.

"What the hell's the plan?" Lance asks.

"I'm sure everyone's not involved in the conspiracy," Melissa says.

Philip eyes the two guys. "They're both involved."

"How do you know?" Melissa asks.

"Oh, that horrible fake tan is just oozing lies."

Melissa grabs the briefcase. She looks at the pilot. "Can you get an encrypted channel back to our home base?"

"Yes, ma'am."

"Radio every pilot you know," Melissa says. "Have them be on standby. Tell them nothing more."

"Roger that, ma'am."

They turn around and approach the military men.

"Let's go. Two more hours and we're evacuating," the tanned military man says.

Melissa nods. "We won't be long."

The military men lead the trio through the doorway. The seal of the president radiates. The halls are empty. Three gray-haired military men look at papers in an office. Two female office assistants shred documents.

The group approaches a control box with the UVASHIELD logo.

"Let's link up here," Melissa says.

She opens her briefcase a crack and hands her smart tablet to Philip.

Lance pops the cover off the wall box. Philip plugs the tablet in.

The military men stare at them.

On the smart tablet screen is "Temperature: 91, Thermal Pressure: 187 PSI."

"The thermal unit looks okay on this one. Let's go to the one down there."

"That's the Offices of the President and the Secretary of Defense," the tanned military man says.

"Based on the heat signatures, that's probably where the busted unit is," Melissa says.

The thick military man flares his nostrils.

Melissa, Philip, and Lance follow the men down the hallway.

Another military man stands at a doorway. He's taller and more muscular than these two. Sweat drips down his face, as he simply stares at the three visitors.

Melissa sees the stout metal door with the seal of the president hanging proudly. Across the hallway and hanging on another door is a similarly prominent seal showing a bald eagle clutching three arrows. Sprawled across the top is "Secretary of Defense."

Melissa takes a deep breath. The air is bitter, hot, full of secrets.

They reach the control box twenty feet down the hall. Lance pops the cover off and Philip plugs in the smart tablet. Melissa grips her case tighter, sweat running into her eyes.

She glances at Lance, who widens his eyes.

Philip swallows hard, loud enough for Melissa to hear.

"Do you want me to storm them?" Lance whispers.

"Look at the size of their guns," Philip says.

Melissa presses a button on the tablet. The screen shows, "Temperature: 93, Thermal Pressure: 156 PSI."

"Ninety-three degrees. Wow, that's hot," Secretary Dunner says.

Melissa, Philip, and Lance turn around. Lance goes for his weapon.

"Ah, Ah, Ahh," Secretary Dunner says, waving his finger.

Lance freezes.

The third guard, the sweaty one, joins his two comrades. The three of them draw their weapons.

"Funny how UVASHIELD stayed in business this long. Its CEO is as dumb as a doornail. Why don't you step into my office?" The secretary opens his door and waves everyone inside.

The military men gesture with their weapons.

Melissa goes in first, still gripping her case. The heat hits her hard.

Philip slides in behind her.

Lance walks in while staring at the tanned military man. "What're you looking at?"

Secretary Dunner goes to sit behind his ten-foot-wide mahogany desk.

Plush blue carpet blankets the office. Photographs of fighter jets, destroyer ships, tanks, and missiles line the walls.

In the corner, President Brooks is bound in the cage, his hands tied to the bars, his mouth gagged.

Melissa looks into his eyes and sees his pain, his suffering, his anger.

The sweaty military man closes the door and seals them all in the office.

"We all need an office pet, right? Some get a fish. Some get a turtle. I got a rat," Secretary Dunner says, snickering.

"Why?" Melissa says.

"That's another dumb question. See, that's why women shouldn't be in charge of companies. Women are only good for making babies, especially in our new society. And I'm glad you three are *not* coming. We don't need any dumb people in the gene pool."

Melissa moves toward his desk. "There won't be any new society."

Secretary Dunner's eyes narrow. "What are you babbling?"

"The thousand survivors. There is no more safe quadrant."

"What are you talking about? You got your little worker ants up there. They're trained to do their mission—your words, not mine."

"They failed. The shields are beyond repair. That's why we're going around to each thermal unit." She lifts her briefcase. "We're trying to eke out any remaining cooling capability in our systems."

Secretary Dunner stands up and studies Melissa's pale face, her sweat-soaked hair, her slow breathing. "You're lying."

"It's true. I have a video from James Wilson's suit that he made thirty minutes ago."

"Where's this video?" the secretary says.

"It's on my smart tablet, which is still attached out in the hall to the control box."

Melissa looks at President Brooks. His eyes are heavy. She looks back at Secretary Dunner.

He starts laughing. "You're either incredibly dumb, or incredibly smart." He shakes his head, and then looks at the sweaty military man. "Go out there and get her tablet."

The sweaty man exits, leaving his other two chums with their guns drawn.

Melissa sets her briefcase down on the desk. "And there's something in here that you must see. There might be a way out of this."

Secretary Dunner rubs his chin. "I'm listening."

Melissa pops open the briefcase. She feels inside past the papers and binders. And then her hand rests on something cold, something hard, something powerful. She removes the pistol.

Secretary Dunner's eyes go wide as he drops down.

Bullets hurl toward Melissa. She falls back, pulling the trigger.

Lance dives through the air and fires lead toward the army men.

Melissa crouches down, hunting for the secretary.

Philip cowers.

The tanned guy collapses with a bullet hole to his head.

The thick guy sends three shots into Lance's abdomen.

Adrenaline pumping, Lance returns two bullets that tear the flesh from the thick guy's neck and steal his life. Then Lance puts the door in his sight.

The sweaty guy kicks it open.

Lance gets two shots off, hitting the sweaty guy's left leg. He topples over and crashes into him.

Melissa crawls around the desk and sees only blood on the carpet.

Lance grabs the machine gun of the sweaty guy, who grabs it back.

"Here," Philip says, sliding a pistol toward Lance.

The sweaty guy regains the machine gun. He aims at Lance's face, resting his finger on the trigger, but Lance gets his shot off first.

The sweaty guy collapses.

"The secretary is gone," Melissa says, crawling back around.

She and Philip go to Lance. He's bleeding out from his abdomen. His breathing is fast. Sweat runs across the stubble on his face. He starts coughing blood.

"Just take slow, deep breaths," Melissa says, applying pressure to his abdomen.

Philip runs to the president and sees a lock on the cage.

The president gestures with his head toward the desk so Philip rushes toward it.

Lance's breathing shallows. More blood oozes from his mouth. His eyes cloud.

Melissa clutches his hand. "Shh, it's okay. It's okay."

Philip finds the key in the desk and runs back to the cage. He opens it and removes the president's restraints and gag.

President Brooks takes a deep breath and puts both hands on Philip's elbows. "Thank you, son."

They both go to Lance.

"It's okay," Melissa says. "You saved the president. You did it."

Blood gurgles from Lance's mouth. "I'm sorry, ma'am... I failed."

"Shh, you're a hero," Melissa whispers, combing his hair with her fingers.

Lance struggles to breathe.

"It's going to be alright." She cradles his head. "Just think of a nice place, with someone you love."

Tears fall from Philip's eyes.

Lance's breathing stops as he cracks a smile. And then his eyes roll back and his body goes limp.

Silence fills the room as Lance's heart now beats through those surrounding him.

"May he rest in peace," the president says.

Melissa stands up and looks at the president with a sad smile.

"Thank you, Melissa. Thank you." He hugs her.

"Thank this man right here," she says, looking at Lance.

"Are you both okay?" the president asks.

"I'm okay," she replies.

"I'm okay, sir, but the secretary is gone," Philip says.

"We have an underground passage. But it's probably boiling down there."

"Should we send someone down?" Melissa says.

"No, he's the least of our problems now. Were you serious about your crew above us?"

"No, sir. As far as I know, they're still up there doing their job."

"I knew you were incredibly smart," he says, his eyes warm and inviting. "Let's move. Others may have heard these gunshots. We need to get the list of survivors squared away." He glances at the clock. "We have two hours left before the doors close, before this heat gets us."

The president goes to the secretary's desk and dials on the phone.

"This is Ross," the phone emits.

Philip raises his head.

"Ross, are you alone?"

"Yes, sir. Secretary Dunner has me shredding papers in the archives."

"The secretary has been relieved of his command. We are enacting Code Yellow."

"Yes, sir," Ross whispers.

The president ends the call.

They all surround Lance's body.

Melissa looks at the UVASHIELD logo on his shirt, stained with blood.

"This man will never be forgotten," the president says. He exhales. "Follow me."

When Melissa grabs her briefcase, she sees her smart phone flashing. The screen reads, "One Missed Call – Dr. Young." She stops breathing.

34

"In God We Trust" is written on a coin. It sits on a pile of thousands of coins pouring out of the back of the shell of an armored truck.

"That's a lot of plays of *Pac-Man*," Chop says, pulling the Rover up to the roadblock.

"We'll have to go around," James says, looking at the craters surrounding the armored truck.

The red blip on the navigation system is only an inch away. Chop accelerates the Rover down a dusty roadway.

"How are you holding up back there?" James says.

Bones grips the extinguisher. Sweat covers his face and his eyes are sluggish. He swallows slowly. "What?"

James rests his hand on Bones' arm. "You okay, man?"

"It's only two hundred fourteen degrees here."

"The sun is setting," James says.

"How are we going to finish?" Chop says. "We have less than two hours. And there are only two of us capable."

James points at the red blip on the navigation screen. "Just get us there." He looks over his shoulder. "How's your oxygen level, Bones?"

"What?"

"Your oxygen level?"

Bones blinks rapidly. "It says four percent."

"We're almost at the shield. You hang in there." James glances at Chop and mutters, "Move it, man."

They approach a crumbled structure. Some bleachers are still visible around a hole one hundred yards wide.

"Looks like a football stadium," Chop says.

Up ahead, there's a metal fence around a one-floor building.

James' pupils dilate as his heart starts racing.

When they pass the building, a hundred yards of open area come into view, covered with dust and stones. A twenty-yard hole is in the center.

"That's probably a soccer field," Chop says.

James stops breathing. The images hit him like a truck with no brakes. He's a boy again, lying on the goal line, feeling the Earth shaking, hearing the people screaming.

"James," a man's voice says.

He's frozen, stuck on the goal line to witness the chaos.

The Earth opens up.

The people on the bleachers scream as they fall toward the hole.

His mother and father look at him for the last time as the Earth devours them.

"James!" the voice says again.

A man in a UVASUIT enters James' vision.

James returns to the Rover, which is stopped outside the field.

Chop peers at him. "Hey, brother. What the hell is wrong?"

"Nothing," James says, shaking his head. "This place just made me think of something."

Chop hits the throttle, launching them forward. Past the field, the shell of an airplane fuselage sits in their path.

"Go around to the right," James says.

"Why?" Chop replies as he follows James' instructions. The trench of a swimming pool is to their left, now half-filled with sand. "Ah, that's why," Chop says to himself.

The red dot on the navigation screen is less than a half inch away.

James looks through the orange haze.

The Rover moves over rocks, shaking the guys.

"Hold on, Bones," Chop says.

Bones braces himself. "I'm still here."

A hundred yards away, the rectangular structure beacons them.

"There it is, Bones," James says. "We found it."

A dozen burned-out cars surround the shield.

Chop rolls the Rover up and backs the trailer twenty feet away from the structure.

He kills the engine. The sound of the stillness scares them.

"I wish these cars weren't here," Chop says. "Too many spots to hide."

James sits up. "Let's just do our best, guys."

James and Chop jump out.

"We'll let you take it from here," Chop says to Bones.

Bones smiles and chuckles. "You guys are always joking."

"How's the suit?" James asks.

"Still at four percent. I hope they leave a few gallons in the tank like they used to in my granddad's old Ford pickup."

Chop and James laugh.

"How's the leg?" James asks.

"It's fucked." Bones holds his head low, his suit shuttering from his tears.

Chop looks around at the abandoned cars.

James puts his hand on Bones' shoulder. "You did good, man. We're going to get you back."

"I'm sorry, James. I'm so sorry," Bones says through his tears. "I didn't mean what I said back there."

James pats his friend on the back. "It's okay. Don't worry about it."

"Sometimes I say shit because I want to sound tough. But I'm really scared. I'm fuckin' scared, man."

"Hey, don't be scared. You just gotta believe that there's something else out there beyond this shithole." James goes over to the emergency pouch and roots around.

"You guys go work. I'll just be here...dying."

"You won't be alone," James says, showing him a cartridge with a label marked, "Jack Daniel's Old Tennessee Whiskey."

Bones' eyes go wide. "Oh, you show me that thing now when I'm dying, you asshole."

James and Chop laugh.

"I didn't even know it was in there," James says.

"See if they have a droid in there for me," Chop says.

Bones chuckles and starts coughing.

James plugs the cartridge into Bones' suit. A ding sounds inside and a message flashes, "Hydration Container 2 Attached." Bones sees, "External Temperature: 220, Internal Temperature: 105, Oxygen Level: 3%." He selects the new hydration container. A straw lowers.

Bones uses all of his energy to suck on the straw. The whiskey floats down and dances with his taste buds. After a half-dozen gulps, he exhales.

"Better than a droid on free-play," Bones says. He grips his extinguisher. "You guys get to work now. No more wasting time," he says with a smile. "I'll be here sipping some Jack and looking for something to kill."

James and Chop go to the shield. The metal has withered to that of thin sheet metal and a hole the size of two basketballs is in the middle.

"Look." James points at a three-foot claw mark on the side.

"I wonder if it sounds like nails on a chalkboard."

They look around at the burned-out cars, a hundred hiding places. Then they look back at the shield.

"How the hell are we going to finish this with just two of us and a cripple?" Chop says. "They're going to shut the doors on the survivors in an hour."

"There won't be survivors if we don't fix this," James says, moving toward the trailer. "Let's get to work."

Chop stares at a deep gouge in the metal.

35

A woman in a red dress lies on the ground. A footprint mars her face. Her mouth opens and closes like a fish. Half her hair has been yanked out and the red dress is torn with half her breasts exposed.

The boy goes to her and sees wires dangling from the back of her head. He kneels down, fixes her dress, and covers her breasts. He looks into her eyes and sees his reflection.

"Don't touch that thing. It's dirty," his mom says.

The boy gives the droid a warm smile, and then scurries toward his mother. They sit down on the side of an overrun bike shop.

Hundreds of people loiter in the streets, some sitting, some lying. The crowd is subdued, surrounded by a sauna. No more screams, no more stones, no more rage fills the crowd.

"Mom, is it ever going to get cooler?" the boy says, sweat drenching his hair.

"I don't know, baby. Don't worry. Whatever happens, I won't leave your side."

The military men stand guard at the fenced area. The workers offering tickets stare at the hundreds of screens all showing the list.

"Look at these fuckin' rats," an older military man says to a younger one.

"Ten more minutes and then we can go to the safe zone, sir," the younger one says.

"What's the point of this when we already know who's going to be saved?" the older one says.

"Secretary Dunner said we must make it look legit."

A whirlwind of heat showers the area. Lights flash. The sounds of engines roar.

The half-dozen military men spread out.

Four helicopters descend. They have UVASHIELD logos on their sides and mounted machine guns.

The voice from a loudspeaker fills the area, "This is UVASHIELD security. Under Executive Order of the President of the United States, you must stand down."

The older military man fires toward the choppers. He runs out in the open, screaming, shooting.

Sparks fly from one of the choppers. Another one returns fire, striking the older military man and sending him down.

The other military men drop their weapons and raise their hands.

The boy stands up as his mother holds him. "Are they here to save us?" he asks with wide eyes.

"Yes, baby," she says.

All the screens go black, and then the image of President Brooks shows. His cheeks are red from the gag. His hair is dusty and the wrinkles in his forehead have aged ten years.

"My fellow Americans. While you have seen your world fall apart for the past eleven hours, I have been held captive by the Secretary of Defense as he attempted a coup of my administration. He had promised certain military officers high-ranking positions in his new government in exchange for fixing the lottery. The secretary has been relieved of his position, and I am now back in control of the government. I am sorry that this occurred under my watch. I am sorry for your pain and for your suffering. I have enacted private security forces from government contractors such as UVASHIELD to disarm the U.S. military and to facilitate those with lottery tickets to enter the safe zone. The corrected, randomized list will be projected on every screen following my broadcast. We are on our last hour, so I ask that you hurry if you have a ticket. Most importantly, please remain calm and follow the guidance of these private contractors, who should be at all lottery posts." He exhales and looks deep into the camera, deep into the eyes of the onlookers. "May God be with us all."

The screens switch to the new list.

Energy flows through the crowd again. The mother and son go into an abandoned clothing store and look at one of the screens.

The mother breaks down as tears flow from her eyes.

"What's wrong, Mom?"

"My baby, you will be saved," she says, holding her son.

He smiles. "Really?"

"Baby, you're going to be alright," the mother says through tears.

"What about you, Mom?" he asks.

She replies with more tears, which turns his smile into a frown.

Through the corridors, two UVASHIELD choppers speed toward an open bay door. A sign reading "To Quadrant 5" is written on the wall. Melissa and Philip are inside one of the choppers as they follow a larger, machine-gun-outfitted security chopper.

People push through a gateway to quadrant 5 as security officers try to direct them.

The choppers zip through the bay door. Down below, hundreds of people shout and cheer.

"Lower us. Over there," Melissa says to the pilot, gesturing toward the lottery station behind a fence.

Four security people in polo shirts hold the fence. Two young workers at the lottery verification system wave at the chopper and hold their hats from the wind.

"There's not enough space to land, ma'am," the pilot says, seeing the crowd surrounding the lottery station.

Melissa grips a container of memory cards. "Just bring me down."

"Ma'am, it's too high. Can you toss it down?" Philip says, seeing the ground twenty feet below.

She slides open the door. The wind blasts her. "There's too much wind," she shouts. "These people need their tickets. This is the last station." She drops a ladder down the side.

"Ma'am, be careful!" Philip says.

Melissa puts the box in her mouth and bites the handle. She moves down the ladder, her high heels catching each step.

One of the workers holds the bottom of the ladder.

Melissa gets ten feet away.

The other worker reaches up as Melissa gives her the container.

"Thank you!" the female worker shouts, smiling.

The chopper bobbles. Melissa loses her grip, hanging on with one hand.

"Steady!" Philip shouts.

Melissa regains her footing and climbs up. Philip leans over and offers his hand.

A gust of wind blows her around.

She grabs his hand and he pulls her inside the chopper.

Melissa looks out and sees the workers configuring the lottery verification system. The security officers allow a man back, then a woman, and then another man. They press their fingerprints against a smart tablet. The workers hand them a card with an American flag emblem.

Melissa looks at a stack of the same size cards secured in a clear box in the chopper.

One of the workers gives her the thumbs up.

Melissa slides the door closed, muffling the wind noise.

"The president is on the screen," Philip says, handing her a smart tablet.

President Brooks stands by his desk in a polo shirt showing the American flag. In the background, Ross packs duffel bags.

"How's it going?" the president asks.

"We just finished delivering the replacement memory cards to the station in quadrant five. Everyone has their opportunity to get their lottery ticket."

"This is good news. Melissa, thank you. America shall forever be indebted."

"I just want to help as many people as possible, sir."

"Go now. There are only forty minutes left. You have passes for your people. Go get your family."

Melissa swallows hard. "I will, sir."

239

"Back home, ma'am?" the pilot says.

"Back home," she replies as he ascends.

"Our hands are in those above us," the president says.

"The report from quadrant two is that temps are dropping. They're up there working. They should be back any time now."

"I will see you over there. My staff is coming with me," the president says as Ross smiles.

Philip smiles inside the chopper.

"My staff, minus one secretary," the president says, ending the call.

Philip sits back as they travel above the crowd. Melissa stares through the window at the dozens of people behind the fence—the dozens of people not getting tickets.

Beyond the crowd, a young girl sits by herself on a chair, surrounded by trash and broken tables.

As they fly by her, Melissa watches her pigtails dance.

36

In the bowels of the underground compound, something climbs a ladder inside a shaft. It is alone, lost, an outcast. Blood seeps from its wounds. The heat has stolen all of its hydration. But it still climbs through the darkness.

A flicker of light reaches the being and shines on the American flag pin on its collar.

On the surface, Chop repositions a piece of steel on top of the shield. James fires his torch to weld the edges. A montage of red, orange, and purple colors in the sky surrounds them under the setting sun.

Chop sees Bones still sitting in the backseat facing forward, gliding his hand in the air, making circles and figure eights, dancing with the colors around him.

James lets up on the flame. "How many more sheets do we have?"

"One," Chop says, looking in the trailer. "Is that enough?"

James tugs on the reinforced shield. "We really should have another half-dozen pieces."

"Hey, this isn't bad for only two of us," Chop says.

"We should already be back now," James says. "Hey, how's your O2?"

"Nineteen," Chop says.

James takes a deep breath. "I'm at ten."

"How's Bones still breathing in there?" Chop whispers, looking at Bones making figure eights.

"Maybe it's the alcohol." James stands up. "Let's get the last piece."

James and Chop walk toward the trailer. They lift the last eight-foot-by-eight-foot piece.

"Steady now," James says.

Chop wavers, dropping it on his foot. He bends to lift it up.

"Watch it, man," James says.

They walk it back to the shield and position it on top of the pile. They take a step back and exhale.

A hissing sound stops them cold as they share a stare.

"What is that?" Chop says.

James sees a pencil-thin line of smoke swirling from Chop's foot.

"Shit!" Chop says.

"I'll get the sealant." James runs toward the Rover. "Bones, where is the sealant?"

Bones still waves his hand.

James searches through the packs, tossing aside tools and cables. "Bones!"

When he goes around to the side, his heart stops. A creature has its head inside a hole in the front of Bones' suit.

James throws a wrench at it. "Get off him!"

The creature erupts from the suit, its lips covered in blood. It hisses.

Three creatures appear from behind a burned-out car, a hundred yards away.

James dives through the air and pounces on the creature, punching it over and over.

The creature tosses James back. It stands over him, hissing, blood dripping from its mouth. It leaps to attack, but James sends a stream of smoke into its body and freezes the life from it.

The creature lands on James' suit, only his glass shield protecting him. He studies its pink, skinless flesh and its jagged, shark-like teeth. But when he looks into its eyes, he sees a glimmer of a soul.

James hurls the creature off.

Chop runs toward him. "They're coming!"

The three creatures charge their way.

"The Rover!" James shouts.

Chop jumps into the driver seat and fires up the engine. Bones is halfway hanging out, his helmet clouded with black char.

"I'm sorry, Bones," James whispers as he pulls him out.

The creatures are thirty yards away.

Chop revs the Rover and takes off.

James jumps inside. He goes in the back to grab the extinguisher, but it falls out. "Shit!"

One of the creatures jumps into the trailer. Another one lunges at him.

James bats it back, sending it tumbling.

Chop runs over mangled metal parts. He swerves and runs over the third creature. The bouncing sends James off the side, only one of his hands holding on.

Chop pulls him in.

"The hill! Go there!" James shouts.

The creature in the trailer jumps into the backseat.

James takes a utility cable and lassoes it around the creature's neck. "Hit the brakes!"

Chop slams on the brakes; both men brace themselves as the creature flies forward, the impact snapping its neck.

The final creature hisses as it closes in on them.

"Go!" James shouts.

The Rover races up the hill.

The creature charges forward.

James looks at it, its eyes burning yellow, its teeth sharp.

The creature is ten feet away on James' side. It lunges into the air.

The Rover launches over the top of the hill. James and Chop fly off and through the air.

The creature reaches for James, but then gravity strikes, sending them tumbling down the hill.

Chop closes his eyes, the impact rattling him.

James bashes into the ground and turns over and over.

The Rover hits hard, its frame twisting. It flips down the hill as tools, packs, and cables explode.

Then the storm ends as stillness ensues.

James opens his eyes, his hips sore, but his mind still alert. He sees Chop twenty feet away so he starts crawling toward him. "Chop!"

The creature is fifty feet in the distance next to the mangled Rover, its axles bent beyond repair.

Chop moves.

"I'm here," James says. "I'm here."

The creature rouses, rolling onto its back.

James sees the smoke escaping from Chop's foot. He reaches him and looks into his helmet. Their eyes meet. "Are you okay?" James asks.

"My arm," he says.

The tape is nearly within reach. James rolls over, grabs it, and then rolls back.

The creature stands up, but its legs wobble like a boxer with a glass chin.

James wraps Chop's foot three times around. He cuts the tape and pulls him up. "Let's go!"

"My arm is fucked!" Chop says.

The creature recovers and trudges toward them.

James and Chop stumble toward the vastness.

"There's nowhere to go!" Chop says.

They move toward the setting sun burning in the sky. The creature hisses, which penetrates their suits, their spines, their souls.

Chop trips and goes down.

James drags him, his muscles on fire, the heat invading his lungs.

The creature is ten feet away and getting closer and closer and closer.

Suddenly, a clank sounds in the distance. A manhole pops open and something rolls out.

James recognizes a human, a man he has seen before; he recognizes Secretary Dunner, covered in blood and sweat.

They look at each other, look into each other, look beyond each other.

A fire ignites in the secretary's eyes, a fire that burns with rage, with evil, a fire that burns hotter than the flames in hell.

The creature runs toward the secretary, pounces on him, and then chomps at his burning flesh.

"Is that…" Chop says.

"Yeah," James replies. "Let's keep moving."

James pulls Chop along as both stumble through the void toward the setting sun.

37

Brian pulls Alex along the corridor. Sweat saturates their shirts. Their lips are crusted and their eyes are half closed.

Richard comes back and puts his arm around them. "Come on, boys. She's almost here."

Janice comes up from the back. "We're saved."

The four pour out onto the landing deck. Three military choppers are parked. A half-dozen military men are handcuffed and are sitting in a holding area behind a fence, guarded by a dozen men and women wearing UVASHIELD security shirts.

Brian sees the colonel in the holding area, and the colonel sees him. "Look at those guys now," Brian says.

"My mom saved the president from them," Alex says.

The colonel looks down at the ground.

The sound of fluttering fills the area. The bay door opens and the two UVASHIELD choppers float inside.

A guy with a headset signals with his hands, directing them toward two open landing bays.

Melissa looks out from the rear chopper and waves.

"There she is!" Alex shouts, running to his dad.

Janice holds Brian as the choppers lower. The wind swirls around, slapping Richard in the cheek, smacking Janice in the neck, pushing Alex in the back, pulling Brian by the hair, yet they all keep smiling.

The choppers touch down.

Philip opens the door as Melissa runs out holding the box of lottery cards. She locks eyes with Alex, and then Richard, a grin on her face. Her skin is pale and her eyes are sunken.

"Mom!" Alex shouts, jumping up to hug her, almost knocking her back.

"We did it," she says, embracing her son and her husband.

When Richard kisses and hugs her, he pulls out a chunk of her hair.

"Mom, your hair!" Alex says.

"God, honey. What's wrong? Did the doctor call?" Richard says.

"Here, Philip. You hand these out. I'll take ours." She opens the box and grabs four of them.

"Yes, ma'am."

"Let's meet here in ten minutes," she says. "We'll all go together."

Philip goes to leave, but then hands her a card. "Mrs. Mercer, you forgot your card."

She accepts it and nods. He scurries away.

"You guys got our things?" she says to Richard.

"Yes, our bags are ready. But, honey, are you okay? God, you're sick."

She rubs his elbows. "Don't worry."

Janice and Brian step over. "You did well," Janice says.

Melissa hands her a lottery card, and then kneels down and gives Brian his. "Your dad did his job. Quadrant two is almost back to normal. Where is he?"

"My dad? He's not here."

Melissa stands up. "They're not back?"

Janice shakes her head, looking at the platform elevator still up at the surface. "There are only thirty minutes left."

"I'm sure he's on his way, the shields in quadrant two are keeping it cool. I'll send up a crew member to check the surface."

"No," Janice says. "Don't risk someone else."

Melissa leans in close to Janice and looks into her eyes. "He'll be back."

38

The sun burns strong. Chop and James stagger past the swimming pool. James looks in and sees sand. Chop only sees the blinding light.

"This way," James says. His suit reads, "Oxygen Level: 8%, Internal Temperature: 105, External Temperature: 236."

"I can't go on," Chop says. "I can't see."

"We have to get back to the cave. We can do it," James says, pulling him.

"We're too far, James. The light is too much. It's stabbing my brain."

"Here, stand behind me," James says. "Hold on to my suit."

Chop follows him. "Hey, remember that story I was trying to tell you before all this?"

"Save your breath, man. It'll be okay."

"That story about working in Vegas."

James licks his crusty lips. "Yeah, I remember."

"I was in Vegas for two years." Chop starts coughing.

James stops.

"Two years," Chop continues. "I knocked this girl up. And I made her... I made her get an abortion."

"Just save your strength."

"I never told anyone this. I was scared. I wasn't ready for a kid. But it haunts me. I killed this baby. God's going to punish me." Chop starts crying.

James turns and puts his helmet against Chop's. He sees Chop's eyes rolled back inside his suit, blood replacing the whites.

"We've all made mistakes, Chop. But I think when something haunts us, it serves as a reminder to strive to do good for others, for our family, for our friends. We've done good out here, man. And I'm not going to leave you out here. We're going to make it."

Chop pats his friend's arms. "This suit's fucked, brother. It must be two hundred inside here. We're fucked."

"We're almost there," James says, helping him move forward.

Minutes of silence go by as both men move with a purpose. They stagger into the field.

James stops as his pupils dilate. He sees the crater in the Earth, the metal bleachers still standing, the goal line now covered by a pile of concrete.

"James," Chop says. "Where are you?"

"Right here," James replies, reaching for him.

"Don't leave me, brother. Those creatures. Are they here? Why did you stop?"

"It's okay. I've got you."

"Where are we?" Chop asks.

"My old school," James whispers.

251

"I can't see."

"There is some shade over there. Maybe I can fix your suit."

"Just don't leave me," Chop says.

"I promise," James replies. He holds on to Chop as they both walk across the field. James can't look, yet he has no choice. He nears the crater.

"James," a whisper enters his suit.

"What's that?" James asks.

"I didn't say anything," Chop says. "Are we almost there?"

James swallows hard. "We're at the center circle."

A flicker of light catches James' eye from the inside of the hole.

"James, down here," the voice continues. "Save us."

James ignores it, moving toward the goal line.

"James. Do something," the voice says. "You just let us die."

"I was scared," James says, tears forming in his eyes.

"What? Who are you talking to?" Chop says.

James keeps moving.

"Are you okay?" Chop continues. "How hot is it in your suit?"

"We're almost there, man."

The goal line is in front of them. A flash of light hits James. He sees himself lying there, frozen, staring at the crowd. James starts hitting his head with his fist.

"What's wrong?" Chop says.

James collapses onto the goal line.

Chop follows him, coughing violently as he hides in the shadow of his colleague, his friend.

James shakes his head. "No. No. I'm okay. Let me see your suit." He checks the seal on the back of Chop's neck.

A flicker hits James' eyes. He ignores it, checking the screws on Chop's suit.

"James," the voice whispers.

James blinks rapidly. A screw is loose on Chop's helmet.

"We're over here," the voice continues.

He looks at the bleachers. His mother and father are sitting there, staring at him.

"What do you see?" Chop says. "Do you see something?"

James widens his eyes. "I see my parents."

"What?" Chop shakes James' suit. "Hey. What's wrong?"

"This is the spot. I was right here. The earthquake. They fell into the Earth right there. I should have tried to save them. But I was so scared."

Chop's body trembles. "James!"

James' parents wave him over.

"Don't be afraid," his mother says. "Save us."

"I gotta save them," James says.

"Don't leave! Don't leave!" Chop shouts, but starts coughing violently.

James stands up and moves toward the bleachers. He sees his mom's smile. Her shoulder-length auburn hair blows in the breeze. His dad stands up, his arms open, his bald head reflecting the sun.

As James nears the bleachers, he reaches for his dad, for his mom. They're right there, inches from him.

"We forgive you, son," his dad says.

James crawls up on the bleachers and lies at his mom's feet, looking up at her as he did as a child.

She stands up and looks down at him, her eyes warm, her smile inviting.

Tears flow down his cheeks. "I'm sorry, Mom. I was scared. I was so scared."

"It's okay, honey."

She lowers her arms, but suddenly, her eyes turn yellow and her teeth transform into daggers.

James blinks his eyes. Two creatures are staring at him, reaching for him. They hiss louder than the cry from a raven flying through the pits of hell.

James rolls off the side of the bleachers. He clamors back, crawling toward Chop, the two creatures staring at him.

"Chop! Chop!" James shouts, shaking him, but his body is lifeless.

"Don't leave me, man," James says, crying.

The creatures creep his way.

James closes his eyes and takes a deep breath, his heart pounding.

"James," a voice says, this time the voice of his wife.

"I'm sorry, honey," he whispers.

"Dad," Brian says.

"Son," James says, tears flowing down his cheeks.

James is back in his apartment, sitting on his couch. Janice walks in. She smiles at him, her eyes warm, her lips plump and covered by a shade of red so vivid that it stops his heart.

Janice approaches him and sits down. Her scent lulls him, seduces him. She leans toward him, the warmth of her body gripping his soul. "Don't be afraid," she whispers.

Brian runs into the room, his hair bouncing. He's holding a soccer ball. His dimples deepen as he jumps toward his dad. James catches him. Brian giggles and hugs his father. "You saved us, Dad."

James takes a deep breath and basks in the moment, a moment so precious that it would forever be with him.

Brian throws the soccer ball into the air.

James looks up at it as the bright light pours in from the ceiling. But then the face of a creature looks down on him and crashes his world.

James is back in the wasteland, the creatures standing over him. He cradles Chop's lifeless body.

"Don't be afraid," his wife's voice whispers.

The creature opens its mouth, its eyes burning. Evil spews from its vocal cords and stabs every muscle inside James' body. The sun burns above the creature, but then the light breaks into a constant flutter.

James closes his eyes, trying to see his family, but all he sees is a black void. His breathing is fast. His heart is pounding.

"I love you, honey," James whispers. "Take care of our son."

The creatures hiss.

James feels something running its claws on his suit. He holds his breath. Something pushes him. His lungs cry, forcing him to gasp air. The burning light finds its way past his eyelids. "No. No. No."

In a burst, James opens his eyes. Three creatures stand over him wearing suits. A helicopter hovers above them.

The monsters from the bleachers scurry away, but the chopper shoots a missile. They explode into pieces, but their hisses linger until the sound of the chopper steals them away.

James shivers as he moves back, his eyes lost in the glimmer of the helicopter.

One of the creatures in the suits puts its hand out. "*Komm mit mir. Sie sind sicher.*"

"What?" James says.

"Are you American?" the suit asks.

"Yes," James replies.

The suited creature raises its hand to its ear. "European One. We have two Americans. One conscious. One unconscious."

"Roger that. Bring 'em aboard."

One suit helps James up. The other two grab Chop's limp body. They move toward the helicopter.

James beholds the thick steel on the chopper, beyond anything he has ever seen. When he approaches the side, he sees a marking, "European Union – Special Recovery Force."

39

The boy lies on the street, hidden behind a metal barrel. His face is red. His eyelids hang closed, his spirit drained.

Dozens of other people lie on the street. One woman waves her hands in the air, dancing with the heat. A man listens to Michael Jackon's "Beat It" on a tiny handheld device. An old lady moans.

The lights flicker, which makes the old lady moan even louder.

A hundred feet away, the boy's mother staggers through the crowd. "Does anyone have another ticket? I have a son. He'll be all alone."

The people ignore her.

She sees a man running through the crowd, wearing a torn T-shirt and cargo shorts. His eyes are wide. His face is withered. His hands are clutching a ticket.

"Sir, I have a son. Can I ask you for your ticket?" she says, grabbing his shirt.

"Get away! There's only fifteen minutes left before they shut the doors," he shouts, running past her.

She falls to her knees and cries her heart out. "Sir, please."

The man keeps hustling, hopping over people like a soldier hopping over landmines.

The mother goes back to her son and breaks down. "Let's get going, baby. They will be shutting the door."

"But, Mom. I don't want to go. I want to stay," the boy says, crying.

"It'll be okay, baby," she says through tears. She picks him up as he cries.

The lights flicker again.

A sudden gust of wind blows heat through the area.

The boy looks up and sees the UVASHIELD chopper racing above him. He connects eyes with Melissa and shares with her his pain, his suffering, his fear.

Melissa holds her breath, a fog of darkness clouding her soul. She looks out at the hundreds of bodies lying in the street.

"Why are they all lying there, Mom?" Alex asks next to her.

"The heat is taking its toll."

Richard, Janice, Brian, and Philip sit around Melissa and her son as the chopper rockets past a sign labeled, "To Quadrant 2."

Melissa cuddles her son; she combs his hair with her fingers and checks his neck and shoulders. "You're getting so big," she says, but then starts coughing.

Richard puts his arm around her. "We're almost there," he whispers.

A tear falls down her cheek.

Janice holds Brian as the chopper approaches the bay door. Brian looks out and sees people running toward the door. "Do you think Dad's down there?"

Janice squeezes him tighter. "Maybe."

Brian sees a pump under the seat. He removes the deflated soccer ball from his bag and grabs the pump.

"What are you doing?" Janice says. "You know not to touch other people's things."

"I need to pump this. Dad is going to teach me," Brian replies with innocence.

Melissa leans over and nods at Janice. "It's okay. Let me help him." The industrial-strength pump inflates the ball in five seconds. She hands it to Brian, who bounces it on the floor of the chopper.

"Thank you," Janice whispers, sharing a smile with Melissa. "Not in here, baby. Sit back." She holds her son as the chopper slows.

The sign above the door reads, "Quadrant 2 Entry."

Hundreds of people chant, trying to push through a turnstile and fence. Choppers and UVASHIELD security officers protect the door. A half-dozen workers use scanners to check in people showing their tickets.

The lights go out in the entryway. The chopper shakes.

"What's going on?" Philip says.

"It's the heat. The lights can't handle it," the pilot says. He brings the chopper down onto a landing zone just inside the fence. The only light in the area is past the bay door into quadrant 2.

The pilot kills the engine.

Philip opens the door. "Okay, everyone, have your ticket ready. You will need to have it scanned before you're allowed entry."

Janice and Brian jump down. "Do you see Dad?" Brian asks, looking at the people on the other side of the fence.

A filthy guy eyes him. "Kid, can I have your ticket? Please…"

"Maybe he's inside," Janice says to her son.

Brian starts crying. "I don't want to go without him."

"I know, baby," she says, tears welling. "Have you heard from them?" she asks Philip.

He shakes his head, sorrow in his eyes.

"Let's go, baby." Janice sees a clock at the ticket station that reads, "0 days, 0 hours, 13 minutes, 29 seconds." "There's still time left. He will come."

As Brian follows his mom to a worker holding a scanner, the ball escapes his hands and bounces toward the fence. He goes for it.

"Brian!" his mother shouts.

The filthy guy snatches it. He smiles, one of his front teeth missing. "I got your ball. How 'bout I trade your ticket for it?"

Janice grabs her son. "Let it go, baby." She pulls him back as Brian stares at the filthy guy bouncing the ball.

The worker scans their tickets and ushers them through the door.

Philip escorts Richard, Alex, and Melissa to another worker with a scanner. She scans Philip's ticket.

Alex and Richard prepare to show theirs, but Alex sees his mom holding back. "Mom, come on."

Melissa kneels down. Tears are running down her cheeks. "I'm not coming."

"What?" Alex says, running back to her.

Janice, Brian, and Philip all watch, their bodies frozen.

Richard joins his wife and his son. "It'll be okay. There is medical care back there."

She stands up as Alex tugs her hand. "I talked to the doctor."

Alex stops pulling and looks up at his mom. Richard holds his breath.

"I have a tumor in my lungs," she says.

"A tumor? What?" Richard says. "There's going to be medical care. They'll help you."

"It's too big, and it's too late. The doctor says I have a few days left at most."

Richard looks deep into her eyes, past the tears, past the redness, past the fog of darkness. He sees something he had first seen ten years ago at the altar, still shining brightly, still warm, still soothing even after all these years of working, of helping others, of solving problems; he sees the beautiful soul of his wife, of his love, of his…everything.

"I can save someone else," she says. "There's still time."

Emotions overwhelm Richard as he holds her tightly and takes a deep breath. His wife flows through his body and into his heart.

"Take care of our son," she whispers softly into his ear.

Melissa kneels down and looks into Alex's eyes. Tears reflect her image. She wipes his cheeks. "Don't cry, honey."

"Why do you have to leave us?" he says.

"When you were born, you almost died."

"What?"

"Your dad and I never told you. During labor, I had a big contraction and your heart rate dropped. The nurses rushed in and tried rolling me from side to side and repositioning my bed, but your heart rate kept dropping. One of the nurses said that you weren't going to make it. And the doctor said there wasn't enough time even for a C-section."

Richard rests his hands on Alex's shoulders.

"But your dad looked into my eyes and said that God wanted us to have a son and that he would be beautiful."

"What happened?" Alex says, swallowing hard.

"Just as fast as you went downhill, you came back. Your heart got stronger. And then you were born. Our baby boy."

"I think I remember that," Alex says.

Melissa and Richard chuckle.

"Your mom will always be here." She puts her hand on his chest. "Always listen to your dad, okay? And keep doing your sculptures, baby. Always do things that make you happy."

"Mom, don't leave," he says, his body shuddering.

"I'll always love you, my son, my baby." She holds him tightly, surrounding him with her soul. And then she sends a whisper of words into his ear, "I will always be with you."

Melissa stands up. "Go now, guys."

Tears filled with sorrow, with pain, with love flow from Richard's eyes. He leans in close to his wife one last time and whispers, "Find me before I turn the corner."

The worker approaches with a scanner. Richard holds his son as the worker scans their tickets.

Melissa steps back.

Brian waves. Janice nods and says, "Thank you."

Melissa nods and gives her a sad smile.

Philip comes over and hugs her. "You're a good woman, Mrs. Mercer. Thank you for finding a way for me, for us, to live. May God bless you."

"Take care of my family," she says.

He starts crying. "I will."

"Someone's looking for you," she says, seeing Ross in the distance at the doorway.

"Where're you going to go?" Philip asks.

She smiles and winks at him. "Go now."

Philip turns and sees Ross. They embrace with a hug.

Melissa steps back, looking at her husband and her son. She goes over to a UVASHIELD security officer. "Can you get me on the other side of the fence unnoticed?"

"You have a ticket, ma'am," he says, seeing it in her hand. "You're going the wrong way."

She smiles at him. "There is no wrong way."

The officer brings her around toward a chopper. She looks back one more time and waves at her son and her husband. She kisses her hand and sends it to them. The light around them glows as they accept her kiss and wave at her. Then she closes her eyes, storing the image of her family in a memory at the front of her mind, where it would stay, where it would always be.

The officer opens the fence on the side.

Melissa sneaks past. "Thank you," she says before coughing violently.

She conceals the ticket and mixes into the crowd.

A man shouts, "They messed up! Let me in!"

Two men try to climb the fence.

"Ten minutes! Ten minutes until the doors close! Anyone with tickets must come through now," one of the officers shouts.

Melissa walks into the darkness.

A woman lies on the street. A man pretends to play a violin.

Melissa clutches the ticket. The boy and his mom move her way.

A fire burns in the mother's eyes, a fire that only mothers have, the same fire that burns in Melissa's eyes.

"We're almost there, baby," the mother says.

"Where are you going?" Melissa asks.

"My son has a ticket. I need to get him to safety."

"Do you need another one?" Melissa says.

The mother stops cold, her pores opening. She turns to face Melissa. "If this is some kind of joke, I—"

"Here," Melissa says, showing it cupped inside her hand.

The mother breaks down and goes to Melissa. "Oh God. Thank you. Thank you."

Melissa kneels down and looks into the boy's eyes. "Don't cry. You and your mom are going to be saved."

Melissa stands up.

"Mom, isn't that woman from the TV?"

Melissa smiles at the mother and says, "Hurry."

"Thank you," the mother says, holding her son.

Melissa watches the mother and son move toward the UVASHIELD security officer. He checks their tickets, and then escorts them through the fence.

Melissa takes a deep breath of heat. She turns and looks into the darkness. Even though there is limited light, she knows exactly where she's going.

40

The British flag proudly displays on the left chest of a woman's polo shirt.

James lies on a stretcher inside an area protected by a clear seal. He wears a T-shirt and shorts with his UVASUIT hanging on a rack behind him. He sucks water from a straw, gulp after gulp after gulp.

The woman checks his pulse as another woman assesses his legs and arms.

Two men stand over Chop's body. One starts an IV, while the other pumps an ambu bag into his lungs. Chop's mustache is flattened.

A tall man with a beard and glasses, wearing a jump suit, walks over to James. "Where did you come from?" the man asks with a thick British accent.

James stops drinking.

"Underground. We're all underground," he says, looking at Chop. "Chop! Can you hear me?" James looks at the man. "Is he going to be okay?"

Suddenly, Chop inhales a deep breath and starts coughing.

James moves off his stretcher and goes to him, looking into his eyes. "We made it. They saved us."

Chop blinks rapidly. "Who?"

"We're part of the European Union," the British man says. "A recovery unit. We thought America was dead."

James looks through the window and sees the cave up ahead.

"Bring us down. I need to get to my family. They're closing the door."

"Bring us down here," the British man says in his headset.

James stands up and looks at him. "We're burning up down there. Our shields are gone. My team was sent up to reinforce the only shields we had time to save, near where you picked us up. But that was to sustain only a thousand people. That's just a fraction of us down there."

"What do you need?" the British man asks.

"Steel," James says. "A shitload of steel. The stuff on the bridge."

"We've been mining that bridge for months now. We can help. We've got two other choppers in the area."

The chopper lowers down near the cave.

Chop sits up. "Go. Be with your family. I'll show them where the shields are. We'll try to save as many as we can."

James puts on his UVASUIT. He walks to the British man. "Thank you. You saved our lives."

"Don't worry. We're here to help. We've got a community above ground in Europe, a pressurized bubble. We're rebuilding."

He goes to leave the sealed area, but turns to the British man. "Oh, one thing. What the hell are those *things* down there? Are they human?"

"Perhaps at one time. They're a mutation, the result of extreme radiation poisoning."

"What do they want?" James asks.

"They want to be like us."

James looks at Chop and simulates twisting his mustache.

Chop grins, and then turns his hairs into curlicues.

The chopper touches the ground. A woman presses a button. Smoke blows down, allowing James to exit the bubble. He sees three motorized bikes near the exit door.

"Can I borrow one of those?" he asks a man in a pressurized suit.

"Sure. Here's the accelerator and here's the brake," the man says, showing him the controls on the handlebars.

"Thank you," James replies.

"We'll see you soon."

James jumps out onto the terrain with the bike. He stands on the pegs and twists the gas. He wavers, but then stabilizes the bike and jets into the tunnel.

Using his heads-up display, he enables the lights on his helmet, which shine onto the rock walls. James zips at thirty miles an hour.

He comes to a split and slows the bike down, looking both ways. The lights reflect off the metal fan blade half-buried in the sand.

At the last moment, he goes left, stones kicking up from the move. James pegs the throttle.

The lights on his suit flicker, and then darkness surrounds him.

He lets off the throttle and punches his helmet. The lights pop back on and reflect off a sign that says, "Return access to underground requires person to be wearing UVASUIT – Press Button from inside UVASUIT for re-entry."

James presses the button. The chain-link doorway opens. He enters and hits the down arrow. The door shuts, and then he descends.

Suddenly, his lungs strain and his chest burns. His suit flashes, "Oxygen Level: 0%, External Temperature: 140."

James gasps, dropping to his knees.

"No. No. No!"

He hits the release buttons under both armpits, opening the suit. The heat finds its way inside him, burning his lungs, strangling him from within.

A light flashes and a buzzer sounds. The word *Depressurizing* blinks. Cooler air blows into the platform elevator.

James struggles, gasping, but then he sucks in a breath of oxygen and extinguishes his lungs. He glances at the countdown timer on his watch: "7:56"… "7:55"…

James gets back on the bike as the platform drops down above the parked choppers. Ten feet from the floor, he twists the throttle and launches off the platform. He hits the ground, rocking from the impact, and then races toward the bay exit.

On the side, the military personnel stand in the holding cell. The colonel gives him a nod.

James squints his eyes and doesn't let up on the throttle.

He slows down near a doorway labeled, "Maintenance Access Only." He swipes his finger on the reader. "Come on! Come on!"

The door opens.

He rockets through a ten-foot-wide passageway at forty miles an hour. At the end of the corridor, he slows down and hits the exit bar on the door.

A wider passageway extends before him. Broken glass and refuse litter the ground. People lie on the concrete.

James knocks over a painted sign that reads, "Haircuts – 28 credits." He dodges a woman, and then speeds between two men showering in the hot air from the turbines.

A sign points to quadrant 4.

James turns and speeds through an open bay door. He enters a common area at full throttle, the people blurring by his view. A hundred yards away a sign says, "Quadrant 2." The thirty-foot door is still open, the door to the survivors.

People sit up. A man cheers. A woman claps.

James' watch beeps. The door starts closing.

He hammers the throttle, the door forty yards away. The UVASHIELD security force guards the fence twenty yards in front of the door.

James hops off the bike.

"James Wilson!" one of the guards shouts. "Let him through!"

James runs through the entryway in the fence and toward the door. "I'm here. I made it."

The clock on the outside reads, "0 days, 0 hours, 0 minutes, 0 seconds." The door shuts and locks.

"It's too late," the guard says.

"It's not too late. We were saved up there. Europe is alive. They're here to help. We're not alone!"

The guard steps back.

James looks through the six-inch-thick window on the door. A crowd of people peers back at him.

"Even if I wanted to open it, I can't," the guard says. "It was triggered to shut automatically. You'd need an override from the President of the United States."

Through the glass, James sees Janice in the group. He starts knocking on the window.

She widens her eyes and picks Brian up, who smiles from ear to ear. "There he is!" she shouts. "James made it! Open the door!"

People cheer around her.

"Janice! Brian!" James says, banging even harder on the glass.

The lights come back. Cool air blows down.

"What's going on?" the guard says.

People rouse from their spots and cheer.

Suddenly, the crowd around Janice and Brian spreads apart. The president steps toward the door with Ross and Philip on his side. Philip holds a smart tablet. It reads, "Temperature in Quadrant 4: 108," but then the number lowers to "100," and then to "90."

"Yes, sir. The temp is dropping." Philip sees "89" on his smart tablet.

"Let's get this door open," the president says.

Two UVASHIELD security officers offer him a smart tablet. He swipes his finger and enters a passcode, and then the door unlatches.

James steps back as the door swings open. The air joins between in there and out here.

The filthy guy kicks the soccer ball to James. "Kick it through the goal!"

James stops it with his foot and bounces it on his knee.

Brian sees his dad and plants his feet, his eyes wide.

James passes it to Brian. "Kick it back, son!"

The ball rolls toward the nine-year-old. He eyes it up and whacks it back with the side of his foot.

James grabs the ball in the air. "Wow! Now *that's* a kick!" He runs to his family, scooping up Janice and Brian.

"You made it!" she shouts, running her fingers through his sweat-soaked hair.

"Dad!" Brian says.

"I made it, guys. I made it." He invigorates his senses. His wife's warmth, her scent, her touch flow through his body and into his soul, removing the pain and suffering which had overwhelmed him. He squeezes his son, feeling his warmth, his energy. James starts crying. "I love you guys. I love you so much."

The president comes over. James puts his son down and tries to hide his tears, but he sees tears in the president's eyes.

"How did you do this?" the president asks, seeing people cheering in both quadrants.

"We're not alone. Europe is alive. They have a colony above ground. They've been here, mining steel. Now they're here to help."

"America is forever indebted to you." The president shakes his hand. "Where is your team?"

"The surface got two."

"What about Chop?" Brian says.

"He's up there now with the Europeans reinforcing as many shields as possible."

Philip checks his smart tablet. "Quadrants two and four are showing sustainable temps."

"What about five?" the president asks.

"It's still at a hundred and twenty."

Richard and Alex come over.

"Thank you," Richard says.

"Your dad is a hero," Alex says to Brian.

James smiles, but then he holds his breath, his eyes wandering. "Where's Melissa?" He sees the boy and his mom crying.

Janice holds on to him. Brian grips his waist. Richard cuddles his son.

Suddenly, trumpets start playing at the beginning of a song. The whisper of Al Green says, "Let's Stay Together."

"Did you do that?" the president asks Philip, who's still holding his smart tablet.

He shrugs.

The song pours out from ceiling speakers and fills the area with life. Everyone stops and bonds together as they sway and sing to the music.

41

Stars blanket the sky. The moon shines brightly. Crickets chirp. The smell of summer humidity swirls in the air.

Melissa takes a deep breath, her eyes half open, the hint of a smile on her face. She looks at the picture in her hand, the picture of her family, and traces the curve of Richard's chin with her fingertip. Then she touches the dimples in baby Alex's cheeks.

A rumble vibrates through the room.

Melissa holds the picture against her heart and follows a shooting star with her eyes, but then the sky flickers as the orange light pushes the stars away.

The couch shakes as light bulbs pop. The heat invades. The pigments of ink smear down the picture and onto Melissa's hands. A blank sheet replaces the image of her family.

The heat singes her hair. Melissa closes her eyes and sees her husband waving, her son crying outside the door to quadrant 2. "I love you," she whispers.

Then the light seeps past her eyelids. She opens her eyes and sees the burning planet above through the ceiling. The viewing filters weaken as the full strength of the light consumes her body.

Her eyes burn out as the ceiling cracks. Fire surrounds her with heat so intense it's no longer heat. Her skin burns and her lungs scream.

Melissa accepts the pain.

It all goes black, and then she opens her eyes.

Melissa sees her book, her sandwich. She takes a deep breath and fills her lungs with cool air. Her skin is soft, healthy. Around her, traffic flows and people walk. The young women sit down next to her with the bags from Victoria's Secret.

She bites her lip and jumps up and over the railing. She runs without looking at the cars and the taxi. She runs with all of her energy to the man, her man, pushing the carriage. She reaches him before he turns the corner.

Richard looks into her eyes.

"Don't go down this way," she says.

"Why?" he asks.

The ground starts shaking. Cars crash. People scream.

Melissa grabs the baby, their baby. She holds Richard's hand and runs away from the turmoil.

"You seem so familiar. What's going on?" Richard says, stopping on the sidewalk, the ground rumbling.

She looks down at baby Alex, squirming in his little bonnet, and then looks at Richard and says, "This is my dream. But this place.

This world. This is different. This is all different. Alex is with us. Maybe we have a chance here."

He narrows his eyes.

She smiles, looks into his eyes, into his soul, and shows him the memories of their life together.

He smiles. "No. This isn't *your* dream. This is *our* dream."

They clutch their baby and run away from the chaos toward the beautiful sun burning in the blue sky.